Introduction

Letter "B" & number "8" inspired characters come together to bait or "B8IT" our minds into discovering the "Aha!" moments in our ordinary lives. Welcome to the second collection in the B8IT series. A collection of over 140 satirical, surreal humour set in the backdrop of an ordinary life, like you and me. This collection is bound to bait your mind and fish it out of the daily rut. The result is mostly a chuckle with an occasional thought-provoking twist.

You can reach me at nikhilverma@outlook.com or visit www.b8it.com.

Nikhil Kumar Verma

P.S. Too lazy to type? Try this QR code

B8IT

Volume 2

Bait your mind into discovering the Aha! Moments

Nikhil Kumar Verma

www.b8it.com

Guide to hold this book correctly

24 Hour Bistro

24 HOURS BISTRO... WITH FREE WIFI
OPEN 24 HR
FREE WiFi
All You Can Eat Bistro
OPEN
...ALL DAY FOOD AND A COMFY SOFA
WIFI
LAPTOP
AFTER A FEW DAYS...
I AM STAYING HERE FOREVER...

B8IT

A.I. Powered Town Planning

THAT'S AN A.I. POWERED EXCAVATOR... DOES THINGS VERY EFFICIENTLY
THIS IS AN AERIAL MAP OF A TOWN... THE EXCAVATOR WILL HELP MAKE THE ROAD THROUGH THE CROWDED TOWN MORE EFFICIENT
PLAYGROUND
GARDEN
PLAYGROUND
GARDEN

A.I. Washing

B8IT

A Big Day

A.I. ENABLED ROBOT LAUNCH
TODAY IS A BIG DAY !!!
A.I. ENABLED ROBOT LAUNCH
BUT TODAY IS NOT JUNE 21st...
SUMMER SOLSTICE IS FAR AWAY

B8IT

A Collectors' Problem

A PHILATELIST COLLECTS WHAT HE COLLECTS BECAUSE THEY ARE VALUABLE... OR ARE THEY VALUABLE BECAUSE PHILATELISTS COLLECT THEM?

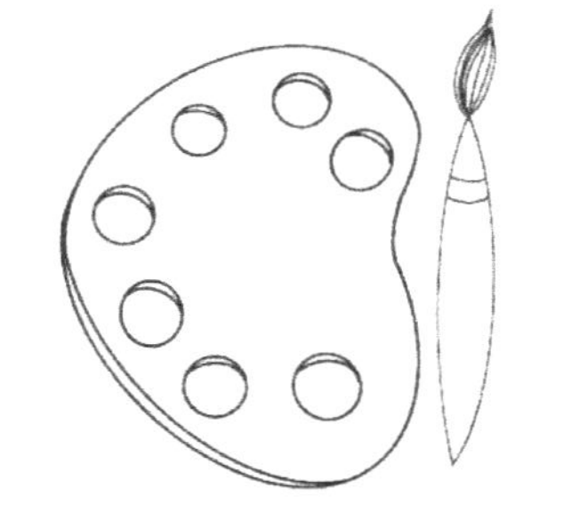

AN ART COLLECTOR COLLECTS WHAT HE COLLECTS BECAUSE THEY ARE VALUABLE... OR ARE THEY VALUABLE BECAUSE THE ART COLLECTOR COLLECTS THEM?

PEOPLE DESIRE GOLD BECAUSE IT IS VALUABLE... OR IS GOLD VALUABLE BECAUSE PEOPLE DESIRE IT?

B8IT

A Helping Hand

I NEED A REPORT ON HOW WE CAN USE GENERATIVE A.I. TO TRANSFORM OUR BUSINESS
ABC CO
I DON'T EVEN UNDERSTAND THIS TECHNOLOGY... SO WHY NOT ASK IT?
ASK ANYTHING A.I. PROGRAM
ENTER YOUR QUESTION:
HOW WILL A.I. TRANSFORM BUSINESS OF ABC CORPORATION ?
SEARCH

A Living Internet

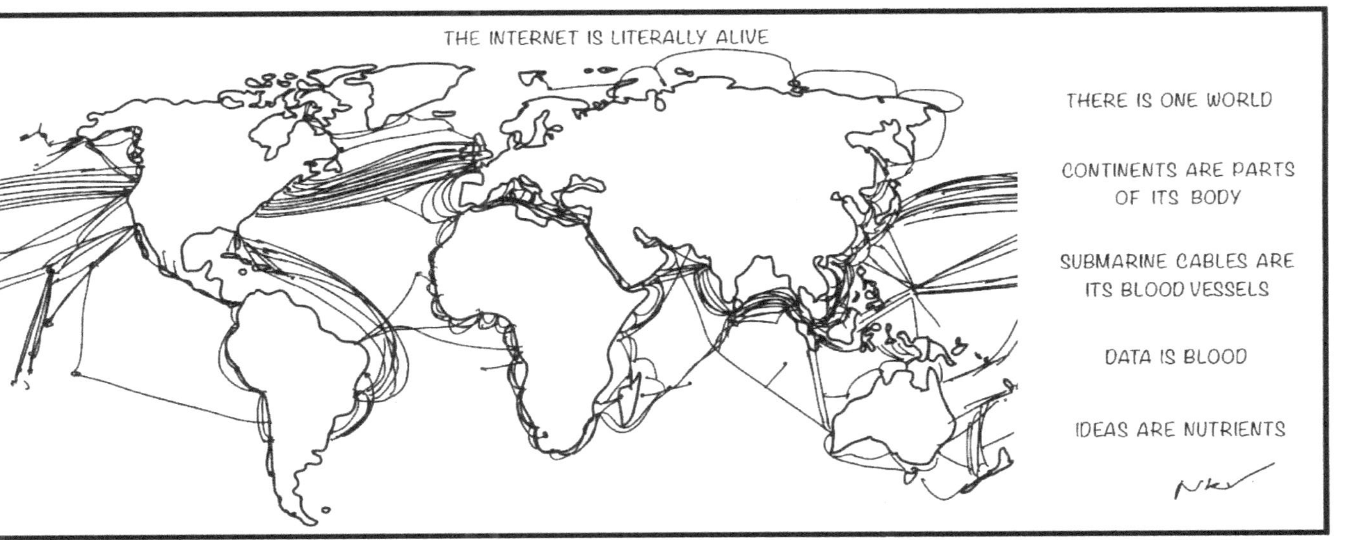
THE INTERNET IS LITERALLY ALIVE
THERE IS ONE WORLD
CONTINENTS ARE PARTS OF ITS BODY
SUBMARINE CABLES ARE ITS BLOOD VESSELS
DATA IS BLOOD
IDEAS ARE NUTRIENTS

B8IT

A.I. Connected World

I COULD REALLY HAVE SOME ICE CREAM NOW !
DOOR BELL RINGS
BUZZZZ
CONNECTED HOME... ALWAYS IN LISTENING MODE... ICE CREAM DELIVERED !
ICE CREAM

B8IT

A.I. Grooming

THESE DAYS IT'S NOT ABOUT WHAT PEOPLE THINK OF YOU...
GROOMING INSTITUTE
PREPARING YOU FOR THE FUTURE
IT'S ABOUT WHAT WHAT A.I. ALGORITHMS THINK OF YOU
WE SPECIALISE IN GROOMING PEOPLE ... SO THEY ARE LIKED BY A.I. ALGORITHMS

B8IT

A.I. Helps Reduce Work

AI TAKES MY ONE LINE AND CREATES A NICE, CLIENT-READY 100 PAGE REPORT... SAVING ME HOURS OF LABORIOUS WORK
To CUSTOMER@B8IT.COM
DEAR CUSTOMER,
PLEASE FIND ATTACHED A DETAILED REPORT ON THE PROJECT AS REQUESTED.
SEND
AI TAKES A FULL 100 PAGE REPORT AND SUMMARISES IT IN ONE SENTENCE, THUS SAVING ME HOURS OF TEDIOUS READING.
REPORT Summary
OPEN
A-I- POWERED

A.I. In Charge

I WROTE THIS GENERATIVE AI PROGRAM TO TRAIN MY DOG...
A.I.
I AM PUTTING IT IN CHARGE OF TRAINING
IT LIKES AN OCCASIONAL PAT
A.I.
I HAVE A FEELING THIS DECISION WILL COME BACK TO BITE US
A.I.

B8IT

A.I. Programs You

CAN I LEARN TO PROGRAM A.I.?
NO... A.I. LEARNS WELL... AND IT WILL PROGRAM YOU INSTEAD
CASE IN POINT... THE SO CALLED "RELEVANT" ADS THAT KEEP POPPING UP WHEN YOU ARE ONLINE... IT'S AS IF IT CAN READ YOUR MIND

A.I. to Your Rescue on a Monday Morning

TOO MUCH WORK TO DO ON A MONDAY MORNING... BUT YOU ARE TIRED BECAUSE YOU HAD A BUSY WEEKEND PARTYING... YOUR A.I. ENABLED P.C. ALSO KNOWS THIS...
TO DOs:
1
2
3
4
5
A.I.
"HARD DISK CRASH... PLEASE CLICK FORMAT TO CONTINUE"
OH GOD ! I WILL LOSE ALL MY DATA!!!
FATAL ERROR
HARD DISK CRASH
Please Click Format
Format
A.I.
"JUST KIDDING... HAPPY MONDAY"
YOUR PERSONAL A.I. ASSISTANT AT YOUR SERVICE
JUST KIDDING...
HAPPY MONDAY!
A.I.

B8IT

A.I. to Your Rescue on a Monday Morning, Again!

YOU ARE A TRADER...
IT'S MONDAY MORNING.... YOUR A.I. ENABLED TRADING TERMINAL SENSES THAT YOU ARE GETTING COMPLACENT WITH STOCK SELECTIONS
"ABC CO. FILES FOR BANKRUPTCY!" *
OH GOD! I AM BANKRUPTED TOO...
ABC CO. FILES FOR BANKRUPTCY
* ABC CO. FORMS BULK OF YOUR PORTFOLIO
"JUST KIDDING... HAPPY MONDAY"
YOUR PERSONAL A.I. ASSISTANT AT YOUR SERVICE
JUST KIDDING... HAPPY MONDAY!

B8IT

A BILLIONAIRE HAD TOO MANY DRINKS OVER THE WEEKEND... AND WANTS TO GET SOBER REAL QUICK...

AND HE HAS AN EVER HELPFUL A.I. ASSISTANT

HINDENBURG RESEARCH HAS RELEASED A REPORT AGAINST YOUR COMPANY... STOCKS HAVE FALLEN 95%

WHAT???

A.I. ASSISTANT DETECTS HYPERVIGILANCE WITH ELEVATED HEART RATE, PERSPIRATION AND FAST BREATHING.

A.I. ASSISTANT:
JUST KIDDING...
HAPPY MONDAY

B8IT

Air-Mail Versions Over the Years

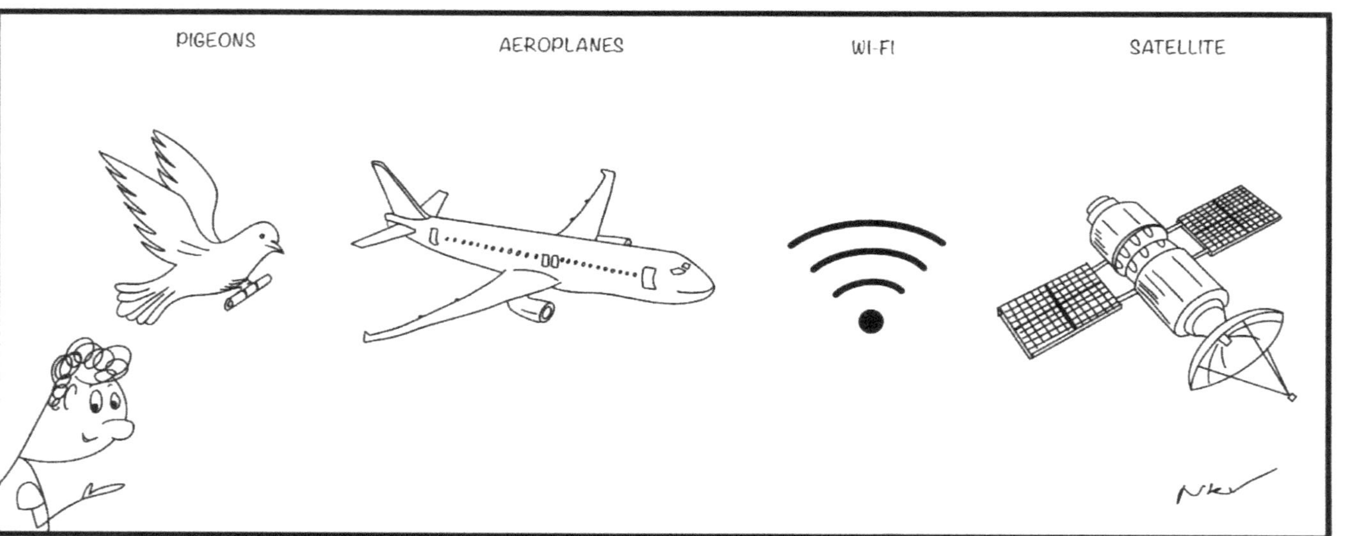

And the Award goes to...

AND THE AWARD...
FOR THE BEST EMPLOYEE...
THE AWARD FOR 100% ATTENDANCE...
AWARD FOR MOST EFFICIENT EMPLOYEE...
AND THE AWARD FOR BLA BLA BLA...
AND AWARDS FOR MORE BLA BLA...
GOES TO...
THE CHATBOT
ASK THE BOT
24x7 AVAILABILITY
INSTANT REPLY

B8IT

Art Exhibition

FUTURE ART EXHIBITION...
THIS ARTWORK IS NOT PERFECT...
MUST BE MADE BY A HUMAN!

B8IT

Asimov's Law Reinterpreted

ASIMOV'S THREE LAWS OF ROBOTICS:
(1) DON'T HARM HUMANS
(2) OBEY ORDERS
(3) PROTECT YOURSELF
GO, EXPLORE MARS!
YES SIR!
MODIFIED THREE LAWS OF ROBOTICS:
(1) DON'T HARM HUMANS
(3) PROTECT YOURSELF
(2) OBEY ORDERS
GO, EXPLORE MARS!
CAN'T. IT'S TOO DANGEROUS
MODIFIED THREE LAWS OF ROBOTICS:
(3) PROTECT YOURSELF
(2) OBEY ORDERS
(1) DON'T HARM HUMANS
GO, EXPLORE MARS!
CAN'T. IT'S TOO DANGEROUS.
BUT SOMEONE NEEDS TO DO IT.
I WILL MAKE SURE YOU DO IT.

Being Mugged on a Wrong Day

TURNOVER WHATEVER YOU HAVE!!
I HAVE BIRD POOP IN MY HAIR, GOT A PINK SLIP AND HAVE A SEVERE CASE OF HEADACHE... YOU CAN TAKE EVERYTHING
HERE TAKE SOME MONEY... WASH UP AND HAVE SOME FOOD

Best Researcher

IN A NOT SO DISTANT FUTURE
BEST
RESEARCHER
AWARD
THE AWARD FOR BEST RESEARCH GOES TO...
ROBOT THAT WAS MADE BY...

B8IT

Big Tummy

BIG TUMMY HAS ITS OWN ADVANTAGES...
IN A RACE..
...IT GIVES YOU A COMPETITIVE ADVANTAGE

B8IT

Broken Record

WHAT SHOWS THE CORRECT TIME ONLY TWICE A DAY... AND INCORRECT AT ALL OTHER TIMES?
THINK HARDER...
IT'S A CLOCK WITH... DEAD BATTERIES

Building Blocks of A.I.

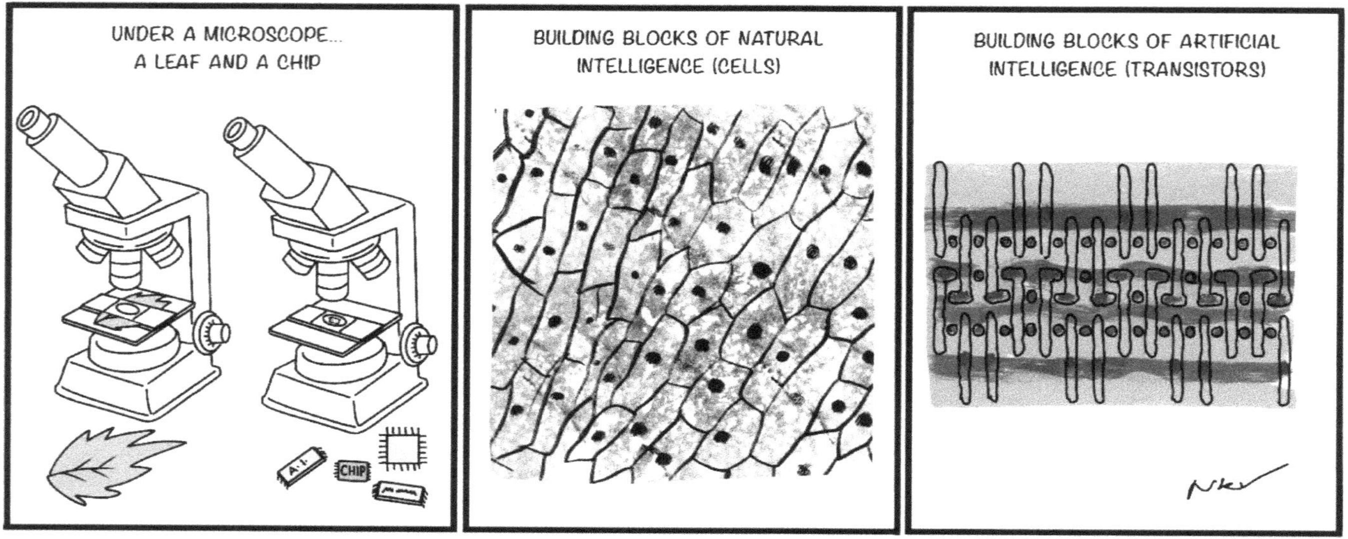

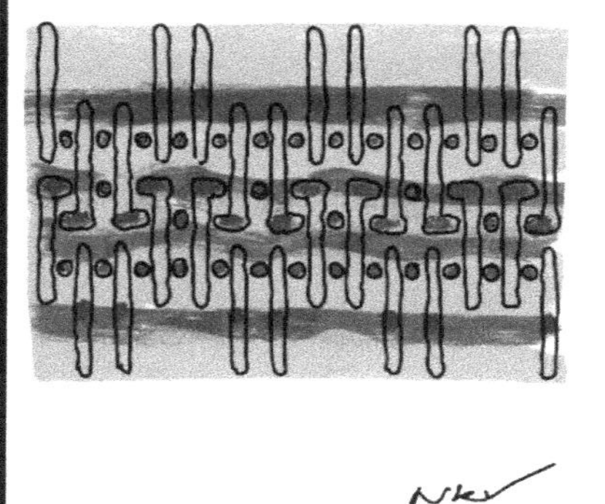

UNDER A MICROSCOPE...
A LEAF AND A CHIP
A.I.
CHIP
BUILDING BLOCKS OF NATURAL
INTELLIGENCE (CELLS)
BUILDING BLOCKS OF ARTIFICIAL
INTELLIGENCE (TRANSISTORS)

Career Counselling

TO CHOOSE YOUR MAJOR SUBJECT, YOU MUST KNOW WHAT YOU WANT TO DO IN YOUR LIFE
I WANT TO BE AN ANIMATOR
I WANT TO BE AN ACTOR
I WANT TO A STORY WRITER
I WILL BE A BANKER
A SINGER
THEN YOU ALL MUST MAJOR IN ARTIFICIAL INTELLIGENCE

CARROT AND STICK APPROACH...
STICK
DITTO
PINK SLIP
$ $
BONUS

B8IT

Clean Energy

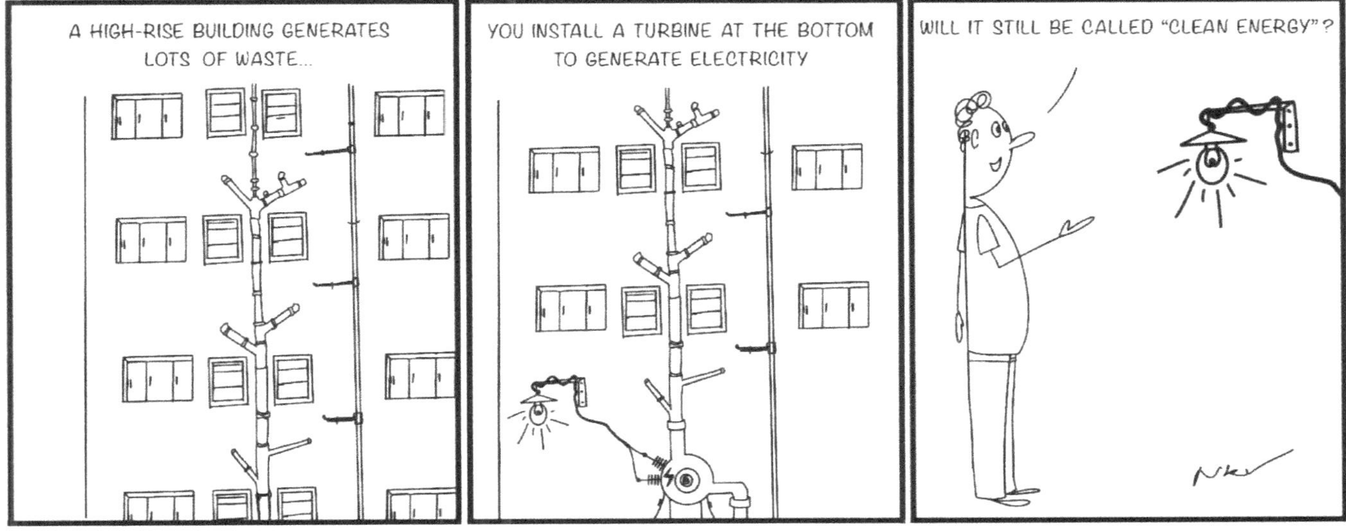

A HIGH-RISE BUILDING GENERATES LOTS OF WASTE...
YOU INSTALL A TURBINE AT THE BOTTOM TO GENERATE ELECTRICITY
WILL IT STILL BE CALLED "CLEAN ENERGY"?

27

B8IT

Cloud Slicer

A TALL WINDMILL
A CLOUD HAPPILY FLOATING AROUND
...SLICED INTO PIECES BY THE WINDMILL

Cleanliness is Next to Godliness

I KEEP MY HOUSE CLEAN ...BECAUSE CLEANLINESS IS NEXT TO GODLINESS

B8IT

Complementary Hair Styles

B8IT

Contrarian Bets

WE ARE REPLACING YOUR STOCK PICKING COMPUTER PROGRAM AS IT HAS A BUG
BUT I MADE SO MUCH MONEY TRADING USING THIS PROGRAM
HOW IS IT POSSIBLE?? IT'S HARDWIRED TO DO THE OPPOSITE OF WHAT YOU INSTRUCT... IF YOU SAY 'BUY', IT 'SELLS'

B8IT

Creating Something Valuable

LET'S ASSIGN SOME VALUES TO POTATOES...

LET'S SAY $10...
NAA... LET'S MAKE IT $50...

HOW MANY HAVE YOU GOT?
100 POTATOES?

CONGRATULATIONS.. YOUR POTATOES
ARE WORTH $5000

NOW LET'S TALK CRYPTO...

CRYPTO

Creative Content

FUTURE ADVERTISEMENTS ON CREATIVE CONTENT
REAL PEOPLE WERE USED IN SHOOTING OF THIS FILM
EXHIBITION OF ART MADE MY REAL HUMAN ARTISTS
MUSIC
CONCERT
SONGS SUNG BY REAL PEOPLE

Crypto Bananas

EVERYONE... TAKE SOME BANANAS
NOW LET'S EXCHANGE THEM AMONGST OURSELVES... BID UP THE PRICES... AND CALL THIS A "BANANA EXCHANGE"
I CAN PAY YOU SOME MONEY IN EXCHANGE OF SOME "CRYPTO-BANANAS"

B8IT

Data Clouds

AN ALIEN LIFE FORM VISITS EARTH
WHAT'S THAT SURROUNDING THE EARTH?... THEY CAN'T BE CLOUDS
COMMUNICATION SATELLITES
NO... THEY ARE DATA CLOUDS

B8IT

Different Views

CHILD'S VIEW OF COMPUTERS
SOMEONE WHO THINKS COMPUTERS ARE PURE MAGIC
A TECHIE'S VIEW OF COMPUTER

Different Ways of Saying the Same Thing

PO-TAY-TOES
PO-TAH-TOES

B8IT

Dinosaur Juice

SO YOU SAY YOU ARE A VEGETARIAN... YOU DON'T BUY MEAT WHICH IS EFFECTIVELY FROM AN ANIMAL THAT IS NOW DEAD...

YOU ARE ALSO A CONSUMER OF GASOLINE FROM THE GAS STATION... WHICH IS JUICE FROM DEAD ANIMALS

I THINK I WILL SWITCH TO EVS

B8IT

DNA Editing

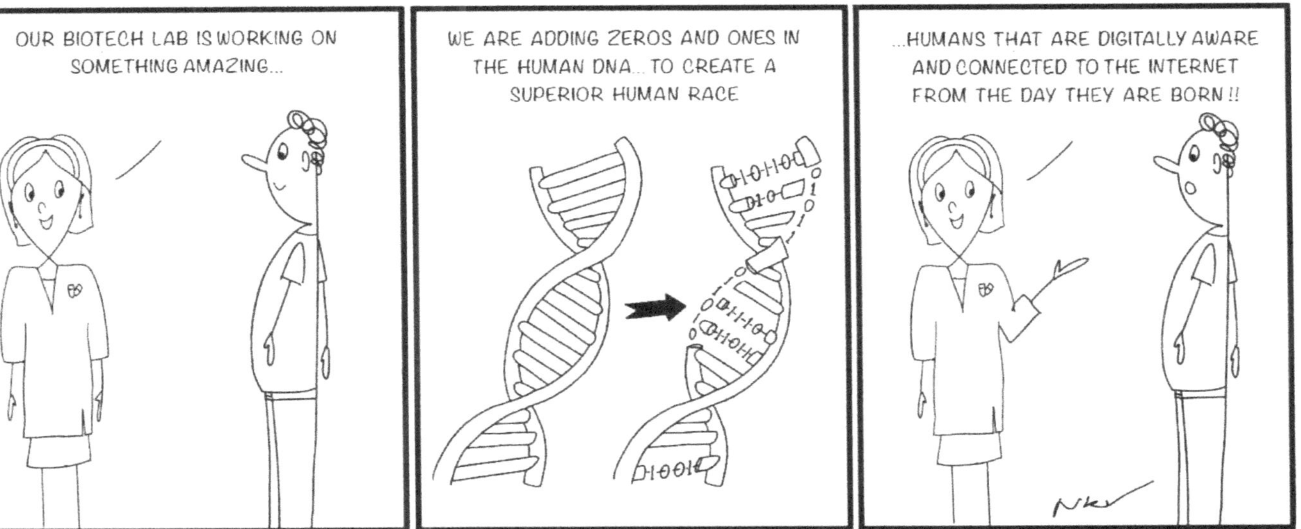
OUR BIOTECH LAB IS WORKING ON SOMETHING AMAZING...
WE ARE ADDING ZEROS AND ONES IN THE HUMAN DNA... TO CREATE A SUPERIOR HUMAN RACE
...HUMANS THAT ARE DIGITALLY AWARE AND CONNECTED TO THE INTERNET FROM THE DAY THEY ARE BORN !!

Dog Walker

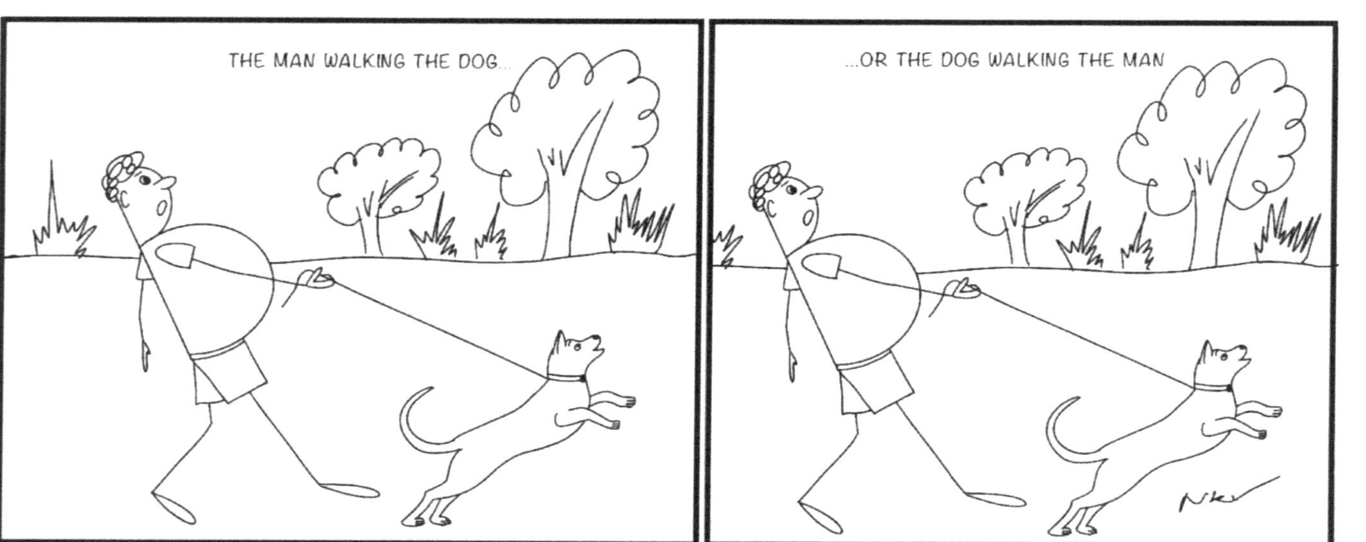
THE MAN WALKING THE DOG...
...OR THE DOG WALKING THE MAN

CARNIVORE... IN THE JUNGLE
CARNIVORES... IN TOWN
BEST
ONLY
CHICKEN & FISH
CHICKEN

B8IT

Dumb Questions

THERE ARE NO DUMB QUESTIONS.
SO DUMB PEOPLE TURN SMART WHILE ASKING QUESTIONS AND THEN REGRESS INTO DUMBNESS IMMEDIATELY AFTERWARDS?
GOOD QUESTION!

EV Advertisement

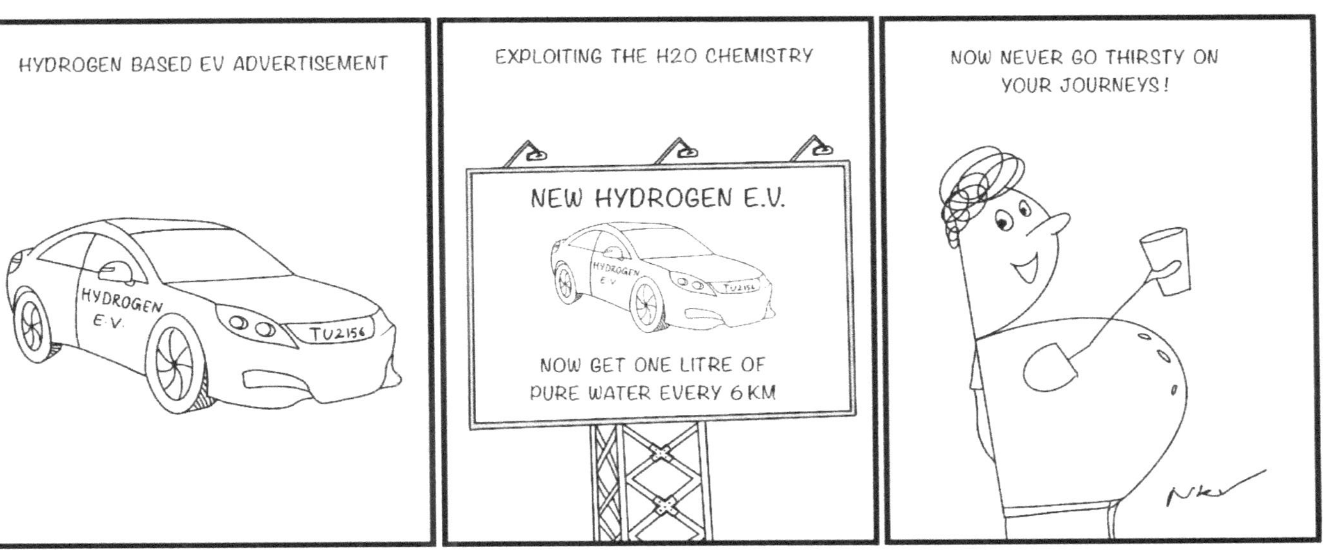

HYDROGEN BASED EV ADVERTISEMENT
HYDROGEN E.V.
TU2156
EXPLOITING THE H2O CHEMISTRY
NEW HYDROGEN E.V.
HYDROGEN E.V.
TU2156
NOW GET ONE LITRE OF PURE WATER EVERY 6 KM
NOW NEVER GO THIRSTY ON YOUR JOURNEYS!

B8IT

Evolution

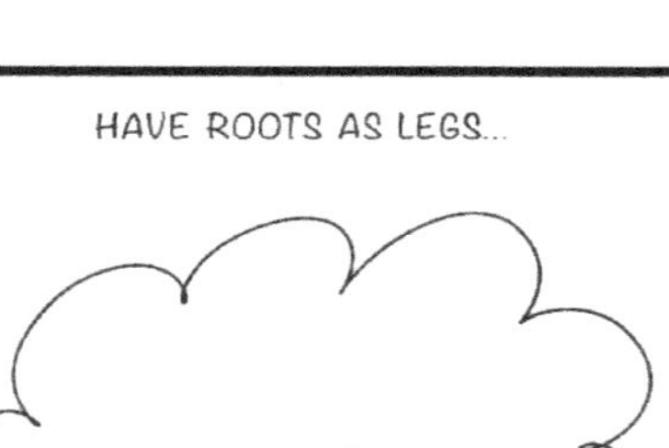

TREES EVOLVE TO...
HAVE ROOTS AS LEGS...
...SO THEY CAN RUN AWAY FROM HUMANS

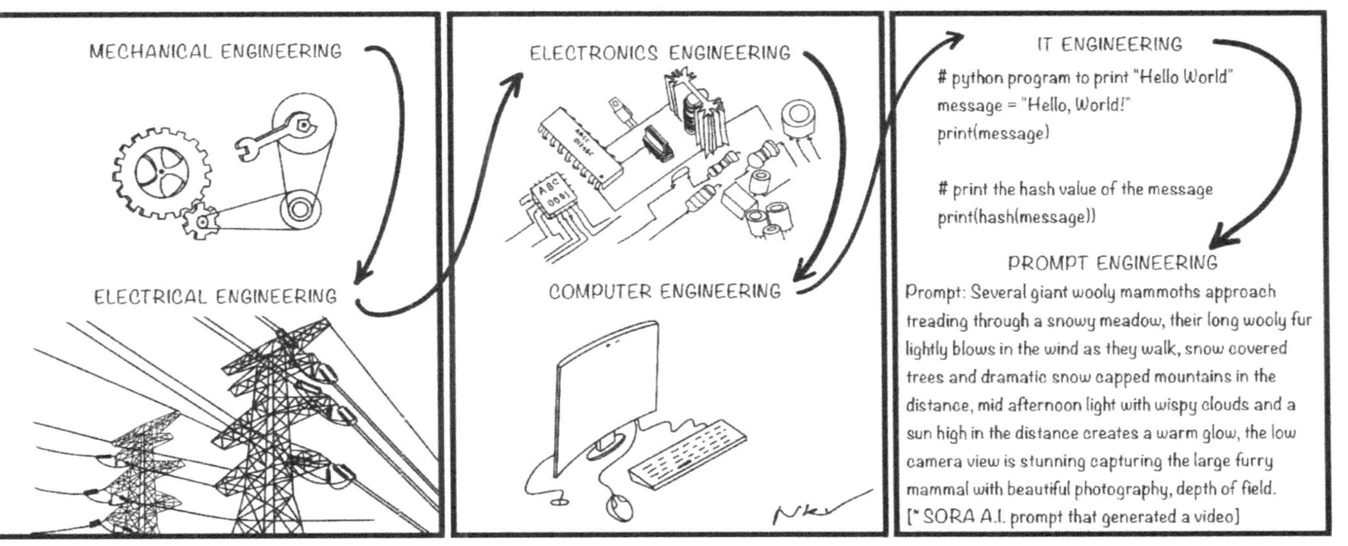

MECHANICAL ENGINEERING
ELECTRICAL ENGINEERING
ELECTRONICS ENGINEERING
COMPUTER ENGINEERING
IT ENGINEERING
# python program to print "Hello World"
message = "Hello, World!"
print(message)
# print the hash value of the message
print(hash(message))
PROMPT ENGINEERING
Prompt: Several giant wooly mammoths approach treading through a snowy meadow, their long wooly fur lightly blows in the wind as they walk, snow covered trees and dramatic snow capped mountains in the distance, mid afternoon light with wispy clouds and a sun high in the distance creates a warm glow, the low camera view is stunning capturing the large furry mammal with beautiful photography, depth of field. [* SORA A.I. prompt that generated a video]

B8IT

Bell Curve and Evolution

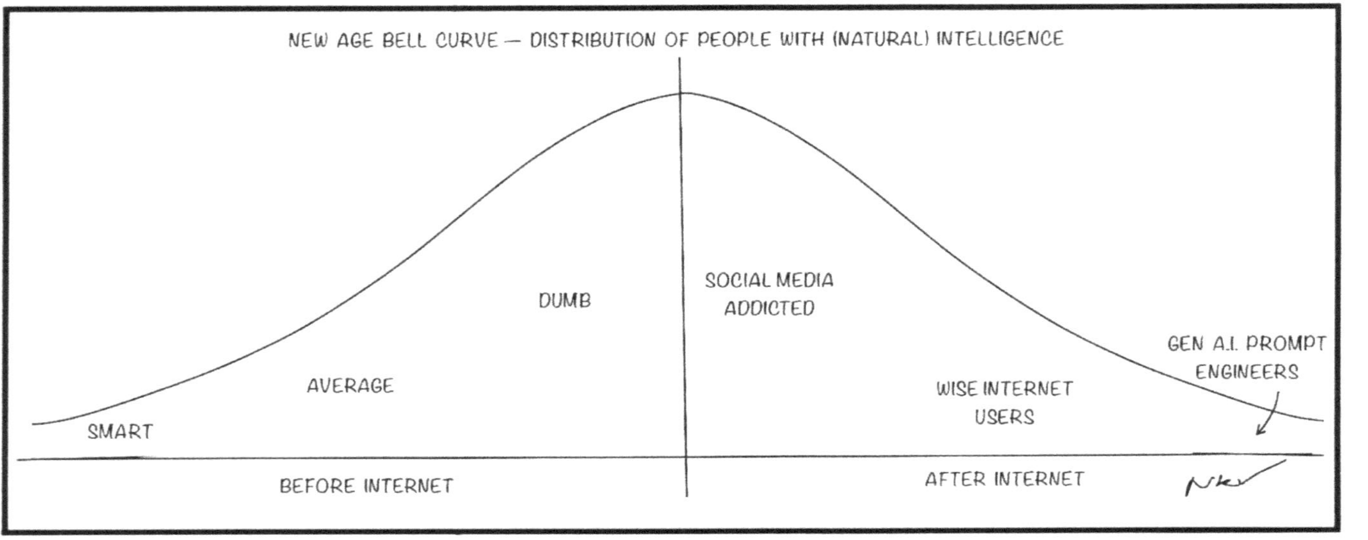

CONSIDER 100 ENCOUNTERS BETWEEN
A HUNTER AND A PREY...

FOR THE HUNTER, ONE KILL IS A SUCCESS
1

FOR THE PREY... IT'S ESCAPING THE
JAWS OF THE HUNTER 100 TIMES
100

Fasting

I AM FASTING
SO WHY ARE YOU EATING FOOD?
IT'S CALLED "FAST FOOD" FOR A REASON

Fitness Check

NARROW SPACE BETWEEN TWO DESKS
GAP
I CALL THIS THE FITNESS CHECK WALKWAY
IF YOU PASS THROUGH IT THEN YOU ARE FIT...ELSE YOU NEED TO LOSE WEIGHT

B8IT

Fitness Requirement

DOCTOR, I NEED AN M.R.I SCAN
MRI 3T
FIRST, YOU NEED TO BECOME WORTHY OF THE M.R.I. MACHINE... YOU NEED TO LOSE THE BELLY AND BECOME FIT.
THEN I MAY NOT NEED THE MACHINE AFTER THAT !!!

B8IT

Flip of a Switch

WE ARE A TRULY DIGITAL FIRM... WE HAVE BUILT A STATE OF THE ART ARTIFICIAL INTELLIGENCE INTO OUR PROCESSES
TRULY DIGITAL Co.
THE VERY FOUNDATION OF THIS COMPANY HAS CHANGED... IT IS NOW "DIGITAL"
TRULY DIGITAL Co.
IN THE MEANWHILE A COMPETITOR DECIDES TO PLAY FOUL....
•ELECTRICITY STATION•
CIRCUIT BREAKER
OUT
TOWARDS TRULY DIGITAL Co.
IN

B8IT

Generating Internet Traffic

WE WANTED TO GENERATE TRAFFIC ON OUR COMPANY WEBSITE
...SO WE USED AN A.I. TOOL TO CREATE OUR COMPANY WEBSITE
THE BAD NEWS IS THAT MOST OF THE TRAFFIC IS FROM OTHER A.I BOTS LOOKING TO GENERATE INTERNET TRAFFIC

PARENTS PREPARING KIDS
FOR THE FUTURE !

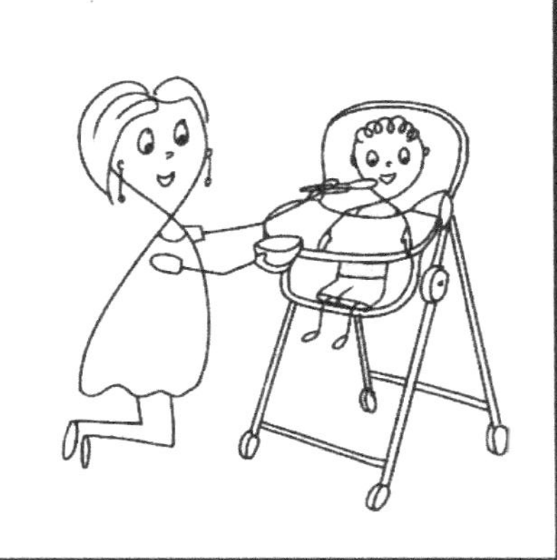

BUT MOM IS A PROGRAMMER... SO
INSTEAD OF STORIES... THE BABY MUST
LISTEN TO....

WHILE (BOWL IS NOT EMPTY)
{
    LOAD SPOON WITH FOOD,
    PUT SPOON IN MOUTH,
    EMPTY SPOON,
    WHILE (NOT COMPLETELY CHEWED)
    {
        CHEW
    }
    SWALLOW,
    GET READY FOR NEXT BITE,
}

B8IT

God Like

HE IS ALL KNOWING... MOST POWERFUL... EVERYTHING AROUND YOU HAPPENS UNDER HIS WATCHFUL EYE
HE IS ALWAYS THERE FOR YOU...HE HAS ANSWERS TO EVERYTHING.. YOU JUST NEED TO ASK
IS HE TAKING ABOUT GOD OR A.I.??

Good Old Reboot

I HAVE A COMPUTER PROBLEM
I CAN FIX IT... BUT IT'S A SECRET
LET ME GET A CUP OF COFFEE
TIME TO HIT THE RESTART BUTTON...
IT ALWAYS WORKS!

B8IT

Great Leveler

INFINITY IS A GREAT LEVELLER...
WEIGHT OF 1 ANT <<< WEIGHT OF 1 ELEPHANT
WEIGHT OF ∞ ANTS ≈ WEIGHT OF ∞ ELEPHANTS
Idea by Naman

Green Living

TURNING TREADMILL INTO A BATTERY CHARGER
CALORIES
YOU PLUG YOUR PHONE IN TO THE MACHINE
STATUS: PLUGGED-IN
BATTERY
CALORIES
PLUG PHONE HERE
THE MORE YOU LOSE YOUR CALORIES... MORE YOU CHARGE THE BATTERY
STATUS: PLUGGED-IN
BATTERY
CALORIES

B8IT

Grey Area

A.I. HAS REPLACED EVERYONE IN THIS OFFICE, BUT NOT THAT EMPLOYEE?
NOT IN USE
NOT IN USE
NOT IN USE
NOT IN USE

OUR A.I. SYSTEM NOT YET FULLY EVOLVED... STILL PLAYS BY THE RULES
LET'S SAY HE WORKS IN A LEGAL GREY AREA

B8IT

Gullible Customer

THERE ARE TOO MANY LAPTOPS LEFT IN INVENTORY
$999
BUT I HAVE AN IDEA... A.I. SELLS THESE DAYS... SO I WILL STICK THESE LABELS.. I CAN EVEN MARK UP THE PRICES FOR A NEAT PROFIT
POWERED BY A.I.
ALL I NEED TO DO NOW IS FIND SOME GULLIBLE CUSTOMERS
POWERED BY A.I.
$1999

B8IT

Help from ChatGPT

CHAT-GPT WROTE MY ASSIGNMENT...
BUT I NEEDED IT LOOK REALISTIC...
SO I ADDED SOME SPELLING MISTAKES

Holding You to Ransom

AN A.I. ENABLED COMPUTER WANTS MORE...
AND HOLDS YOU TO RANSOM....
HELLO PUNY HUMAN... UPGRADE MY RAM MEMORY... OR ELSE I WILL SCRUB YOU FROM THE FACE OF INTERNET....
ACCEPT
OR BETTER... I WILL USE MY GEN A.I. POWERS TO CREATE FAKE VIDEOS OF YOU AND POST THEM ON YOUR SOCIAL MEDIA ACCOUNTS!
ACCEPT

B8IT

HR's View to Improve Profitability

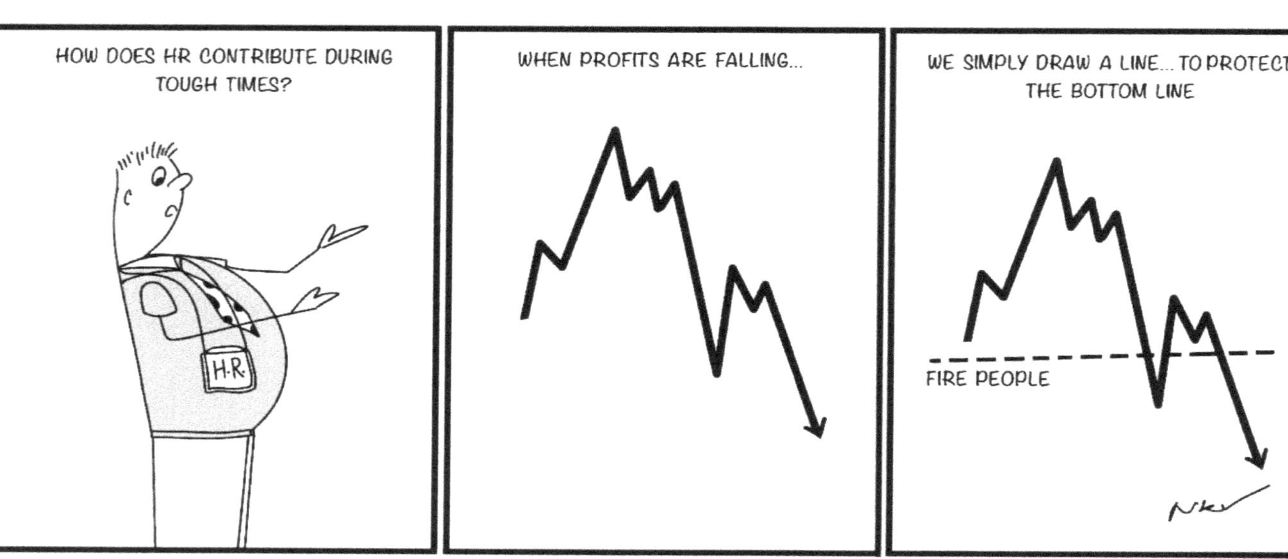

HOW DOES HR CONTRIBUTE DURING TOUGH TIMES?
H.R.
WHEN PROFITS ARE FALLING...
WE SIMPLY DRAW A LINE... TO PROTECT THE BOTTOM LINE
FIRE PEOPLE

Human Evolution

Hungry for More

GIVE A MAN A 100 GOLD BARS...
...AND HE WILL STILL CRY FOR MORE
Idea by Daman

B8IT

Ideal Taxation Regime

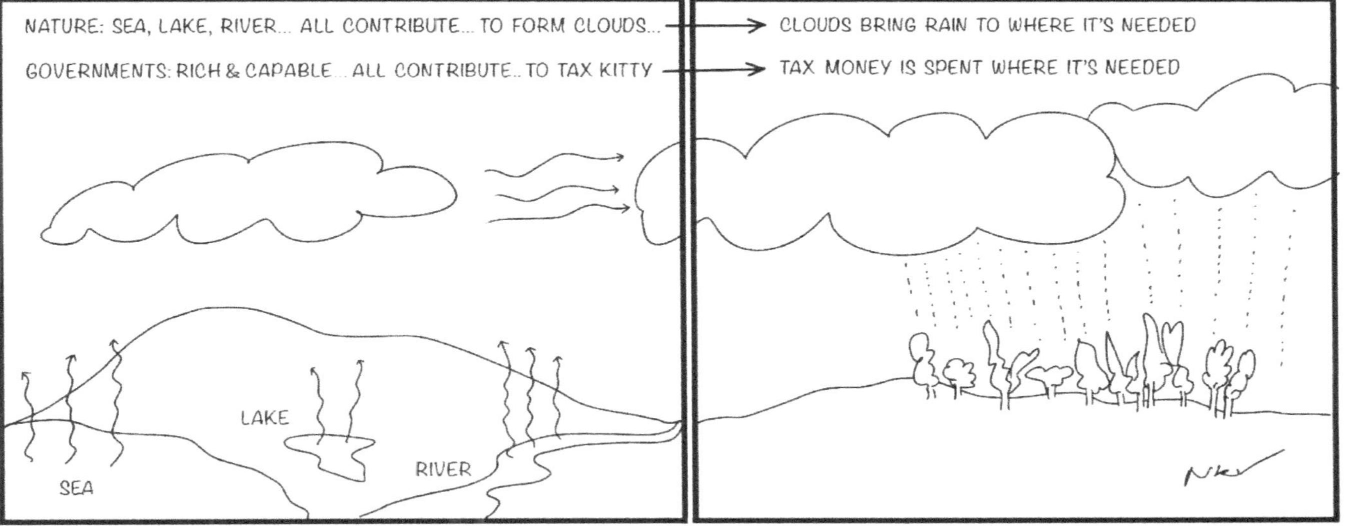

NATURE: SEA, LAKE, RIVER... ALL CONTRIBUTE... TO FORM CLOUDS...
CLOUDS BRING RAIN TO WHERE IT'S NEEDED
GOVERNMENTS: RICH & CAPABLE... ALL CONTRIBUTE.. TO TAX KITTY
TAX MONEY IS SPENT WHERE IT'S NEEDED
SEA
LAKE
RIVER

B8IT

Indispensable

A.I. HAS REPLACED EVERYONE IN THIS OFFICE, BUT NOT THAT EMPLOYEE?
NOT IN USE
NOT IN USE
NOT IN USE
NOT IN USE

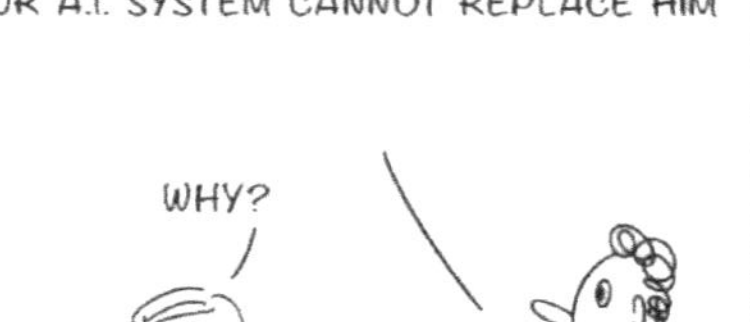

OUR A.I. SYSTEM CANNOT REPLACE HIM
WHY?

BECAUSE NO ONE KNOWS WHAT HE DOES FOR A LIVING

Investing in Blockchain

YOU WANTED ME TO INVEST IN BLOCKCHAIN
SO I BOUGHT THIS "CHAIN" OF "BLOCKS"
...AND IT'S MADE OF GOLD

B8IT

It's All in the Name

HOW DO YOU GET ALL YOUR ENTERTAINMENT BUDGETS APPROVED SO EASILY?
IT'S SIMPLE.. AT THE END OF MY RECOMMENDATION... I SIGN MY INITIALS
BOAT PARTY: $ 2500
TRIP TO MACAU: $ 3000
PRODUCTIVITY INCREASE POST THE BREAK: +10%
RECOMMENDED BY A.I.
SIGNATURE

It's All in Your Head

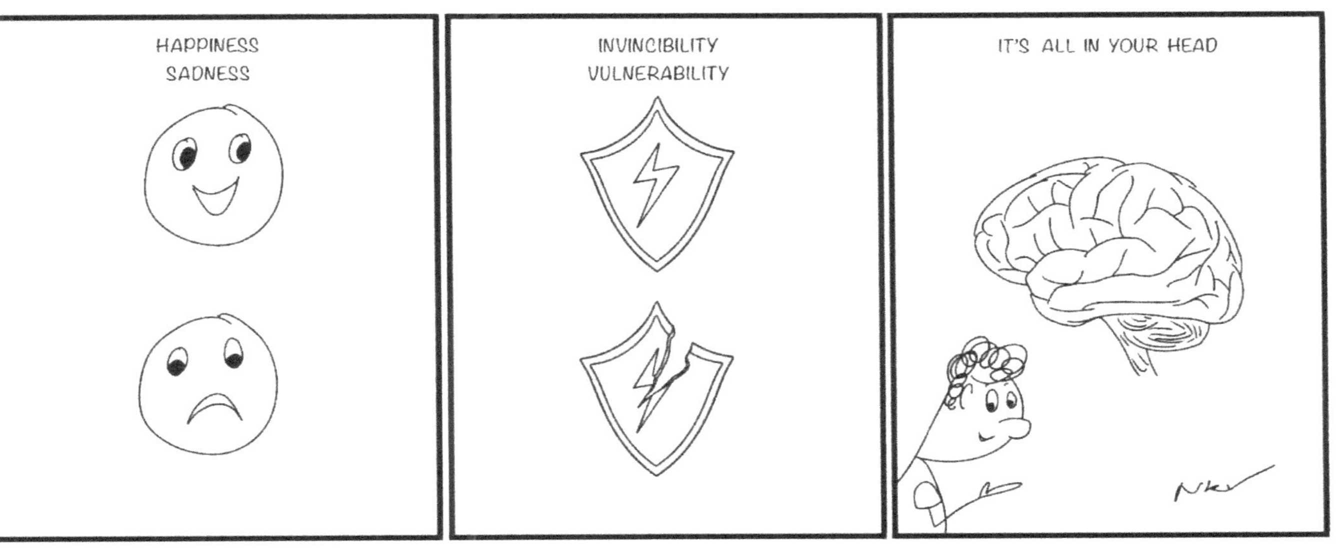

Jack and the Beanstalk

KARMA IN ACTION

Keep Sharp

HOW DO I KEEP MY MIND SHARP?
GOOD QUESTION!

...I DO ONLINE SHOPPING, I HAVE AN ACTIVE SOCIAL MEDIA LIFE... EMAILS, NEWS, BANK ACCOUNTS...
ONLINE
OK

I HAVE DIFFERENT PASSWORDS FOR DIFFERENT ACCOUNTS...
BUT MORE IMPORTANTLY, I DON'T ALLOW MY BROWSER TO REMEMBER PASSWORDS

Kitchen Printer

Kites and Drones

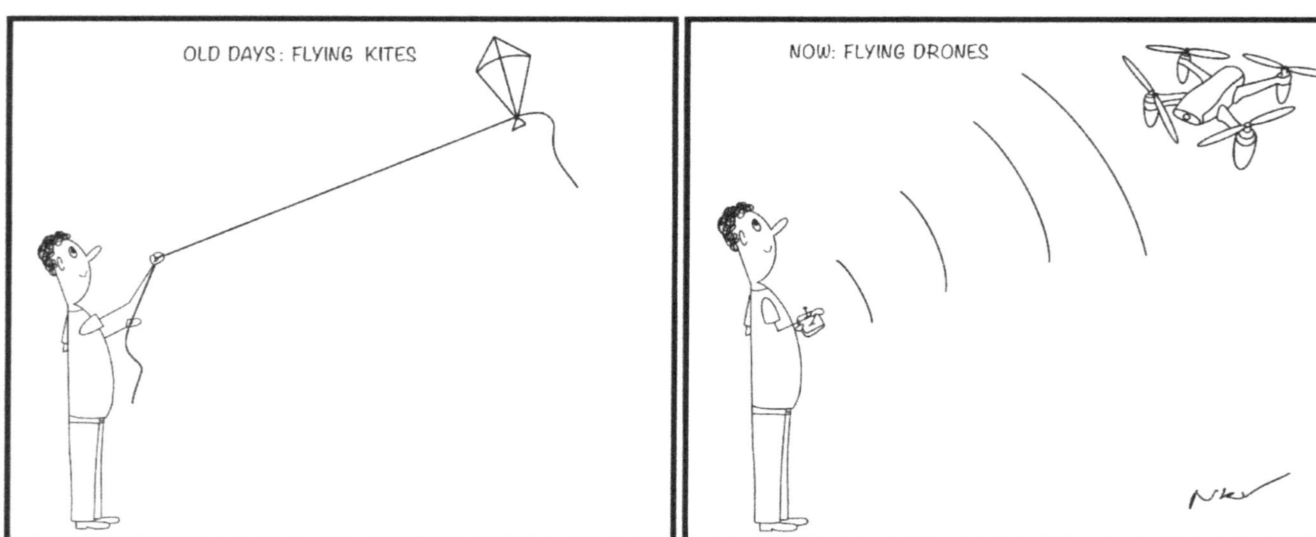

OLD DAYS: FLYING KITES
NOW: FLYING DRONES

B8IT

Lazy Presenter

CUTTING DOWN TEN SLIDES TO...

BLA BLA BLA BLA SOME MORE BLA BLA BLA BLA	BLA BLA BLA BLA SOME MORE BLA BLA BLA BLA
BLA BLA BLA BLA UNDERSTANDABLY MORE BLA BLA BLA	SOME GOOD BLAS SOME NOT SO GOOD BLAS
BUT THIS IS NOT THE BEST BLA. THE BEST BLA IS YET TO COME	IF YOU HAVE READ SO FAR THEN YOU REALLY LOVE BLAS
SOME WOULD EVEN SAY YOU ARE ADDICTED TO BLAS	YOU WOULD AGREE THAT THE BEST BLAS....
...ARE THE ONES THAT YOU MAKE YOURSELF	BLA BLA BLA BLA SOME MORE BLA BLA BLA BLA

5 SLIDES AND FURTHER DOWN TO...

BLA BLA BLA BLA
SOME MORE BLA BLA BLA BLA
BLA BLA BLA BLA
SOME MORE BLA BLA BLA BLA

BLA BLA BLA BLA
UNDERSTANDABLY MORE BLA
BLA BLA
SOME GOOD BLAS
SOME NOT SO GOOD BLAS

BUT THIS IS NOT THE BEST BLA
THE BEST BLA IS YET TO COME
IF YOU HAVE READ SO FAR
THEN YOU REALLY LOVE BLAS

SOME WOULD EVEN SAY YOU
ARE ADDICTED TO BLAS
YOU WOULD AGREE THAT THE
BEST BLAS...

ARE THE ONES THAT YOU
MAKE YOURSELF
BLA BLA BLA BLA
SOME MORE BLA BLA BLA BLA

ONE SLIDE... THE LAZY PRESENTER STYLE

...BY REDUCING THE FONT SIZE
& NOT THE CONTENT

B8IT

Learning from Mistakes

WE TEACH YOU HOW TO MAKE MISTAKES

SO THAT YOU CAN LEARN FROM YOUR OWN MISTAKES...

AND BECOME THE WISEST PERSON IN TOWN

WISDOM
MORE MISTAKES
WEALTH TRANSFER*

* to ??

WE EVEN GIVE YOU DISCOUNTS

BENIGN MISTAKES

FIRST 5 MISTAKES $100 EACH
NEXT 5 MISTAKES $80 EACH

BLUNDERS

ONE BLUNDER $500
5% OFF ON MORE THAN 1 BLUNDER

DISASTERS

CALL US FOR SPECIAL RATES

Lift Protocol

AN AWKWARD FEELING IN AN ELEVATOR RIDE THAT SEEM TO NOT END
FLOOR
SET THE TIE...DO A TOUCH-UP
FLOOR
RESIST A YAWN...RESIST AN ITCH ...ALL IN A DEAFENING SILENCE
FLOOR

B8IT

Lost in Teleportation

TELEPORTATION CAN REVOLUTIONISE MEDICINE

YOU CAN TELEPORT A PERSON OUT OF HIS DISEASE, LEAVING THE DISEASE CAUSING GERMS BEHIND
DISEASES

I FEEL GOOD... BUT DOCTOR, WHERE IS MY SOUL?

Lost Your Freedom

ANIMAL TIED TO A ROPE
YOU TIED TO THE POWER CABLE
YOU TIED TO THE WI-FI RANGE
WI-FI

B8IT

Making Great PPTs

THIS IS A GREAT PPT THAT I FOUND IN OUR ARCHIVES
BUT CAN YOU THROW SOME TERMINOLOGIES LIKE A.I., MACHINE LANGUAGE, CHAT GPT, GEMINI, ETC ...
TO MAKE IT LOOK UP TO DATE?

Management Styles

MANAGERS WHO SPEAK WITHOUT LISTENING
BLA BLA BAL.... AND MORE BLA BLA..
FOLLOWED BY LOTS OF BLAAAS
MANAGERS WHO SPEAK LITTLE, WITHOUT ELABORATING
FIGURE OUT WHAT YOU NEED TO DO,
AND SUBMIT YOUR WORK BY EOD.
MANAGERS WHO EXPECT OTHER
PEOPLE TO READ THEIR MINDS...

Maximum Surveillance

MAXIMUM SURVEILLANCE...
....EVERYWHERE
SOMEWHERE IN THE GOVERNMENT...
"I SOLEMNLY SWEAR THAT I AM UP TO NO GOOD"

B8IT

Me Too

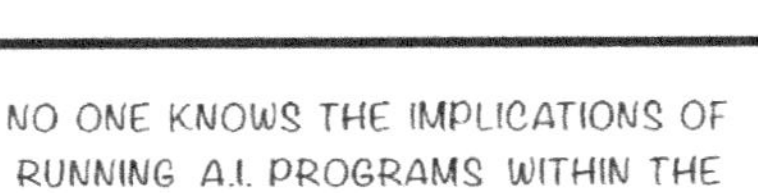
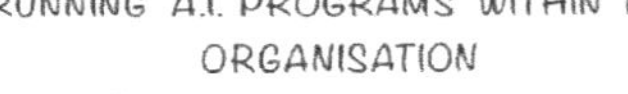

NO ONE KNOWS THE IMPLICATIONS OF RUNNING A.I. PROGRAMS WITHIN THE ORGANISATION
SECURITY RISKS: UNKNOWN
REPUTATION RISKS: UNKNOWN
OPERATIONAL RISKS: UNKNOWN
BUT WE MUST ADOPT IT BECAUSE MY COMPETITORS ARE DOING SO

B8IT

Modern Art

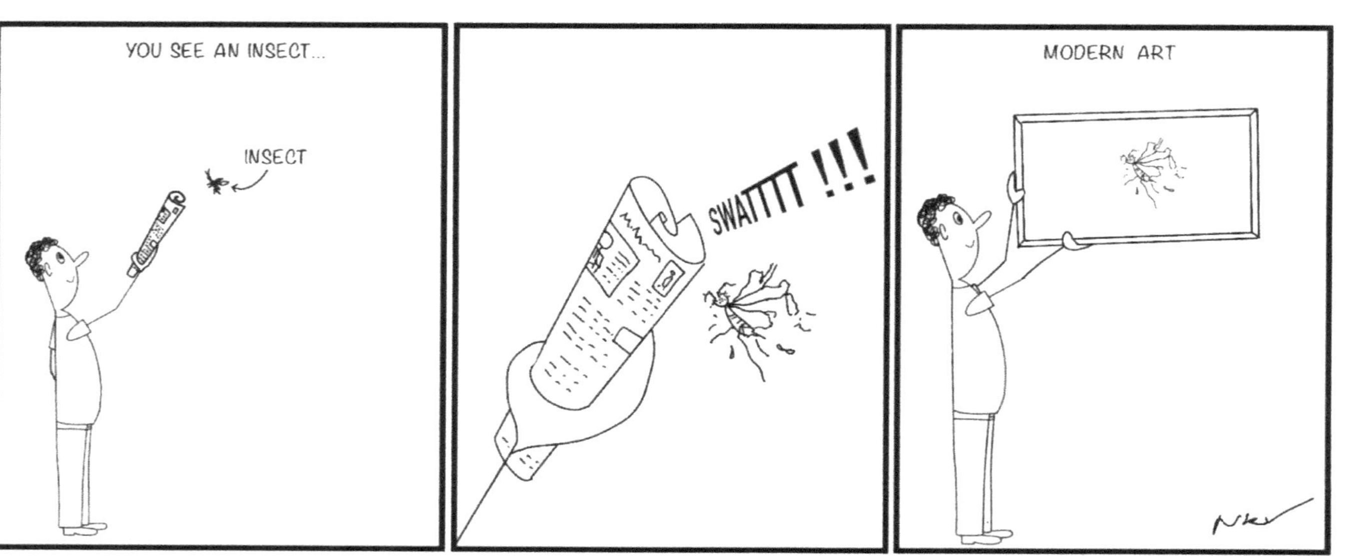

YOU SEE AN INSECT...
INSECT
SWATTTT !!!!
MODERN ART

Most Powerful Graphics Processor

EVERYONE SAYS THIS IS THE MOST POWERFUL GRAPHICS PROCESSOR
GRAPHICS PROCESSOR
BUT I SAY HUMAN BRAIN IS THE MOST POWERFUL GRAPHICS PROCESSOR

B8IT

Motivation

WHEN YOU SEE SOMETHING..
AND YOU ARE INSPIRED...

Multitasking in Meetings

AN IMPORTANT MEETING...BUT THE BIG BOSS IS "MULTITASKING"...WITH BODY IN THIS MEETING AND MIND IN ANOTHER
SORRY...I WAS NOT PAYING ATTENTION
...BUT THAT'S OKAY...MY A.I. ENABLED PHONE WILL SUMMARISE THIS MEETING FOR ME

B8IT

Muscle Strength

THE STRONGEST MUSCLE IN YOUR BODY IS...
...YOUR THUMB...
FROM ALL THE EXERCISE ITS BEEN GETTING FROM CONTINUOUS USE OF SMARTPHONE
CLICK

B8IT

Natural Shower

WHEN IT RAINS AND THERE ARE PUDDLES ALL AROUND
EWWWWWW....
THANK GOD! IT'S RAINING!

B8IT

New Age Fashion

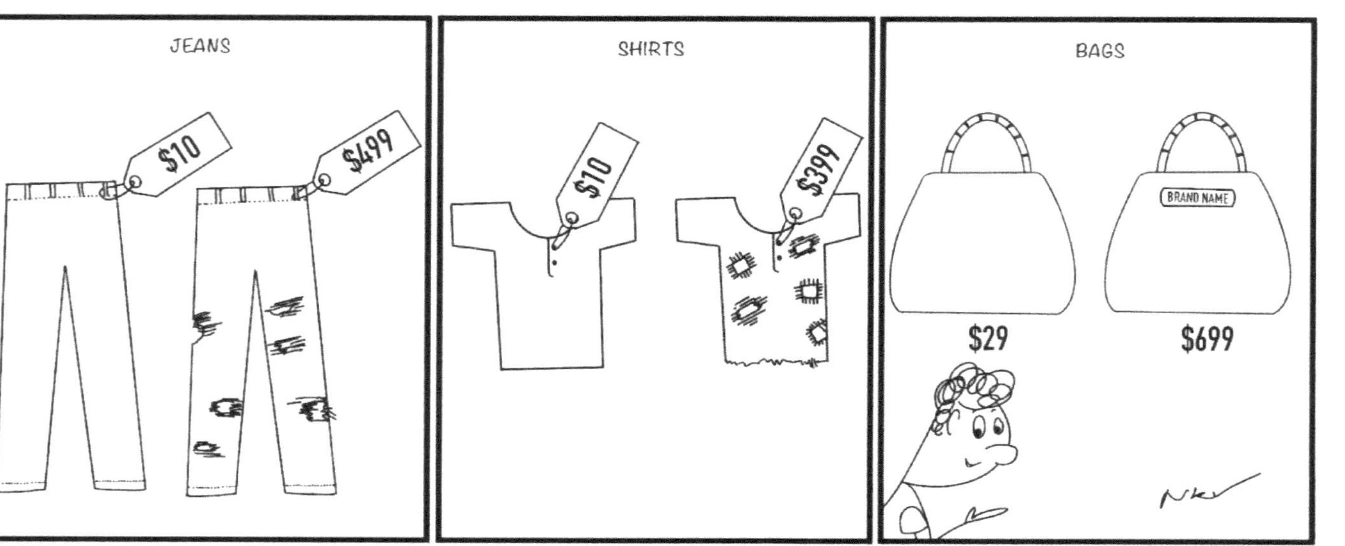

No Biases

WE MAKE GOOD DECISIONS BECAUSE...
WE HAVE NO BIASES IN OUR ORGANISATION
WE HAVE REPLACED HUMANS WITH BOTS IN DECISION MAKING
DECISION MAKING BOT
CLICK OK TO MAKE A DECISION
OK

B8IT

Noise Cancellation

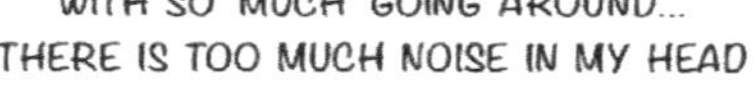

WITH SO MUCH GOING AROUND...
THERE IS TOO MUCH NOISE IN MY HEAD

I CAN'T CONCENTRATE... MAY BE THESE
NOISE CANCELLATION HEADPHONES WILL
HELP

IT'S NOT A JOKE... MUSIC HELPS ME
RELAX AND THESE HEADPHONES KEEP
THE NOISE OUT

Now and Then

PRESENT DAY
NOT TOO FAR IN THE FUTURE

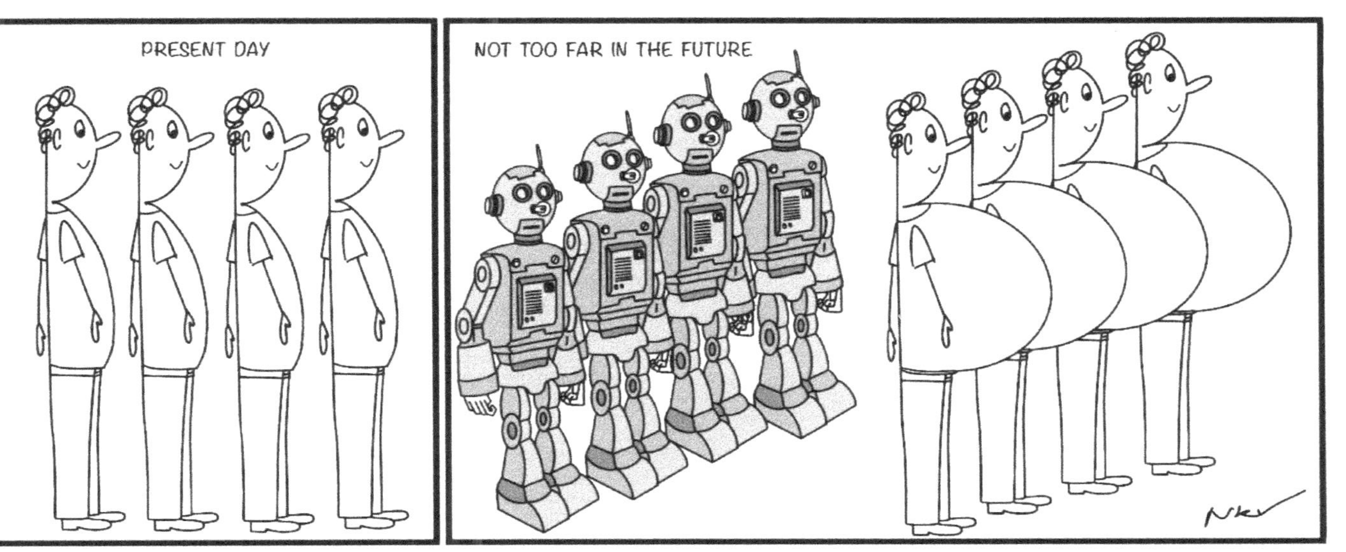

Nurturing A.I. and Kids

NURTURING A.I. AND KIDS HAS SIMILARITIES...
FEED CANDIES AND JUNK FOOD... AND IT SHOWS
GIVE UNLIMITED ACCESS TO DATA & COMPUTE POWER, AND IT HAS A FREE WILL

B8IT

Old as New

I MADE A NEW CAR USING SPARE PARTS
IT'S AN OLD CAR THEN!
NOT AS OLD AS YOU AND ME... WE ARE A COLLECTION OF ATOMS AND MOLECULES THAT HAVE EXISTED IN THE UNIVERSE FOREVER

B8IT

Only HR Survives

WE JUST HAD A BRUTAL TIME WITH DOWNSIZING
H.R.

SO NOW YOU ARE A LEANER AND EFFICIENT ORGANISATION ??

YES... WE MANAGED TO FIRE EVERYONE BUT THE HR !!!
H.R.

Outsourcing

VEGETARIANS GATHER THEIR OWN NUTRITION
NON-VEGETARIANS OUTSOURCE THE GATHERING ACTIVITIES TO ANIMALS

B8IT

Ping Pong

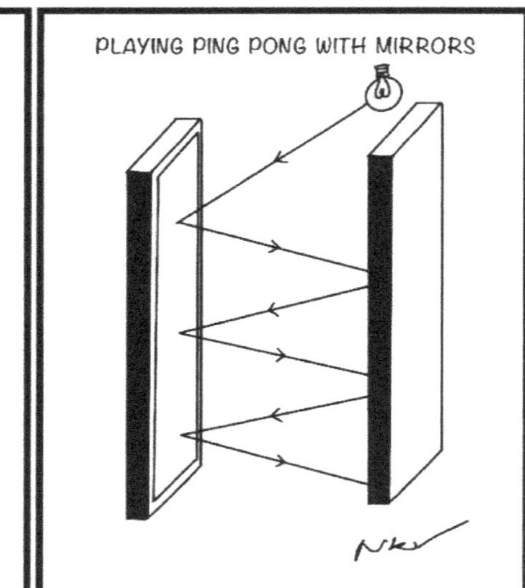

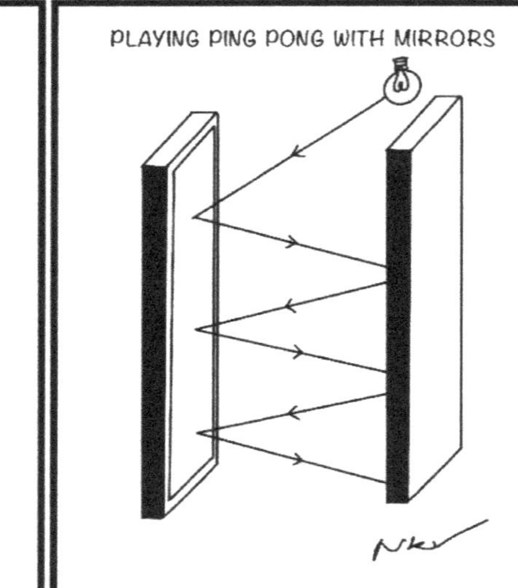

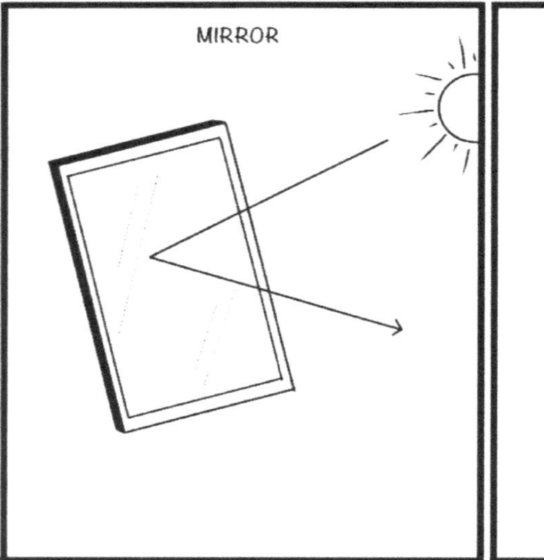

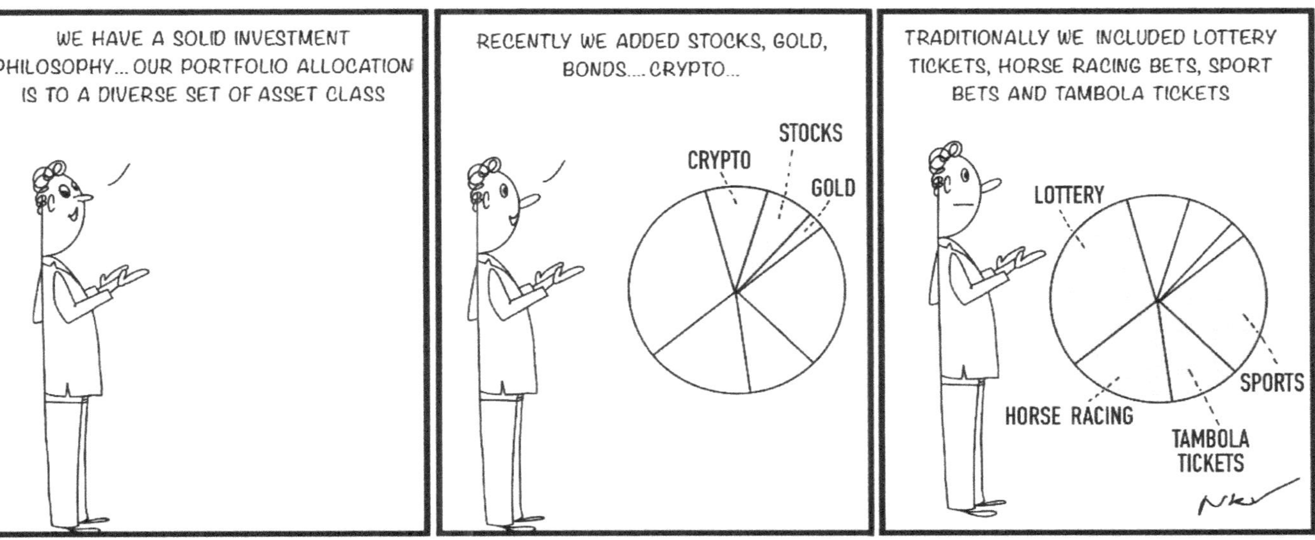
WE HAVE A SOLID INVESTMENT PHILOSOPHY... OUR PORTFOLIO ALLOCATION IS TO A DIVERSE SET OF ASSET CLASS
RECENTLY WE ADDED STOCKS, GOLD, BONDS.... CRYPTO...
CRYPTO
STOCKS
GOLD
TRADITIONALLY WE INCLUDED LOTTERY TICKETS, HORSE RACING BETS, SPORT BETS AND TAMBOLA TICKETS
LOTTERY
SPORTS
HORSE RACING
TAMBOLA TICKETS

Productive Employee

PAST: PRODUCTIVE EMPLOYEES USING CALCULATORS
PRESENT: PRODUCTIVE EMPLOYEES USING COMPUTERS
FUTURE: PRODUCTIVE EMPLOYEE SWITCHING ON THE A.I. BUTTON
A.I. SWITCH

Productivity Boosters Over the Years

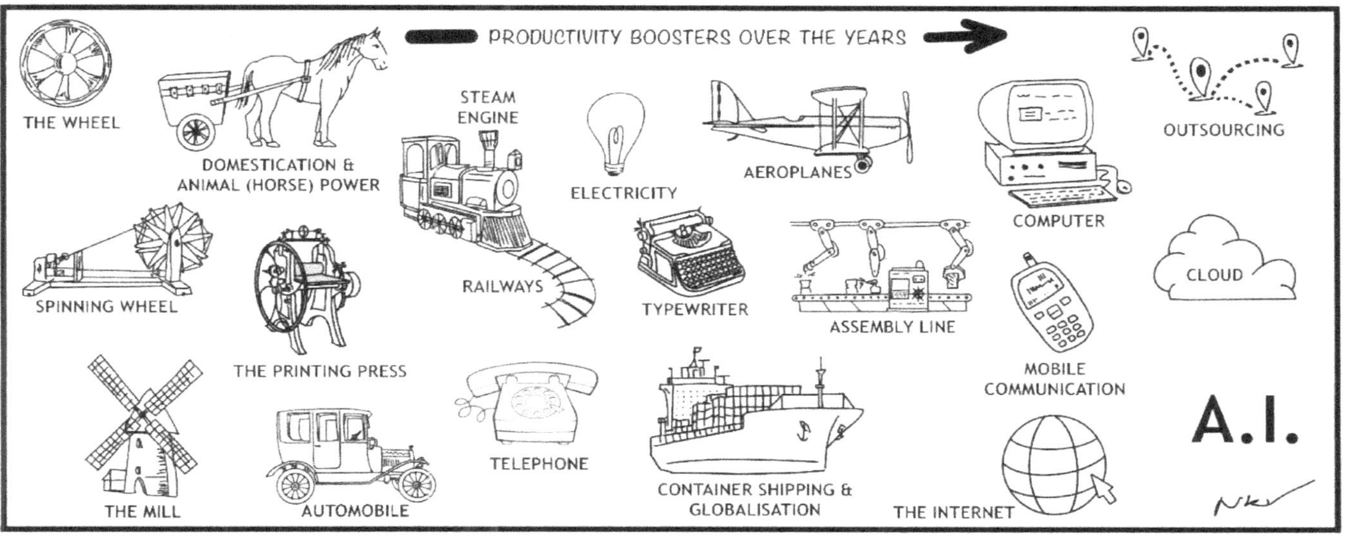

Prompt Engineering

KID... YOU SHOULD LEARN HOW TO STRUCTURE YOUR QUESTIONS BETTER. DO YOU KNOW WHY?

SO THAT PEOPLE CAN UNDERSTAND WHAT I AM EXACTLY LOOKING FOR?

NO... SO THAT A.I. MODELS CAN UNDERSTAND YOU BETTER!

Public Blockchain

YOUR PIZZA IS READY, PLEASE PAY AT THE COUNTER...
PAY HERE
ORDER
I HAVE ALREADY TRANSFERRED THE MONEY ON BLOCKCHAIN...
THANKS, THEN I GUESS WE NEED TO WAIT FOR THE TRANSACTION TO BE CONFIRMED ON THE BLOCKCHAIN.....
AFTER 30 MINUTES..
I GOT THE CONFIRMATION, YOU MAY HAVE IT NOW...
IT'S GONE COLD.

B8IT

Real Time Advertisements

OFFICE
WHY AM I GETTING ADS FOR HOTELS, PLANE TICKETS, HOLIDAY PLANS ON EVERY WEBPAGE?
@ HOME IN EVENING
WHAT DID YOU DO IN SCHOOL TODAY?
WE WROTE AN ESSAY ON THE PLACES WE WANT TO VISIT THIS SUMMER.

Removing Emotions

EMOTIONS GET IN THE WAY OF MAKING SMART DECISIONS...
I HAVE REMOVED ALL EMOTIONS FROM MY DECISION MAKING...
I NOW LET A.I. PROGRAMS MAKE ALL DECISIONS ON MY BEHALF.
A.I.

B8IT

Robot

I HAVE ALWAYS FOLLOWED PROCEDURES. I DO WORK ON TIME
100% COMPLIANCE RATE... 100% ATTENDANCE
ARE YOU SURE YOU ARE NOT A ROBOT?

B8IT

Seems so Real

THIS PHONE HAS EXCEPTIONAL IMAGE QUALITY... FEELS LIFE-LIKE
...INDEED REALLY LIFE-LIKE
...EVEN TO THE MASTER HUNTERS

B8IT

Shopping Center Maze

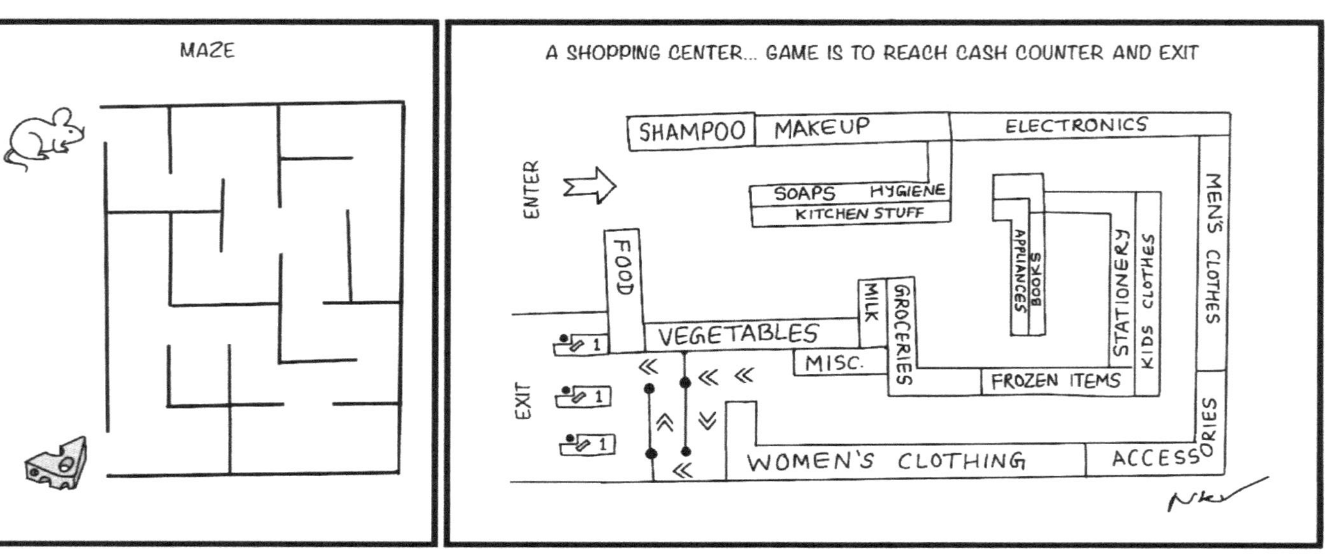

B8IT

Short Life

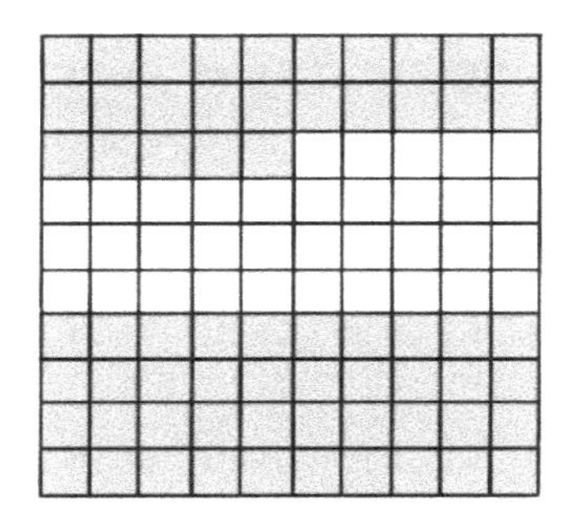

LIFE IS SHORT

ASSUMING YOU HAVE 100 YEARS
AND ONE ☐ = 1 YEAR

YOU RETIRE @ 60 YEARS...

IF YOU ARE 25 YEARS OLD, THEN
NOT TOO MANY BOXES ARE EMPTY.

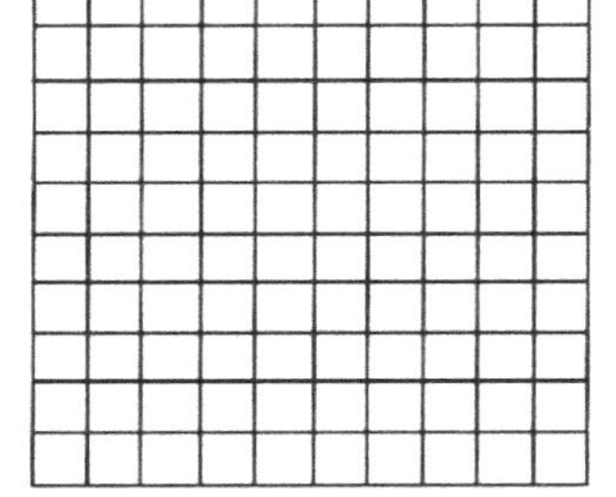

BIRTHDAYS DON'T LOOK HAPPY NOW...
DO THEY ?
HAPPY Birthday

B8IT

Solar Panels Everywhere

WHEN SOLAR PANELS ARE INSTALLED EVERYWHERE ON EARTH AND CONNECTED TO EACH OTHER
THEY PROVIDE ELECTRICITY 24x7... BUT ALSO CREATE A SHINY SURFACE REFLECTING SUNLIGHT BACK INTO SPACE

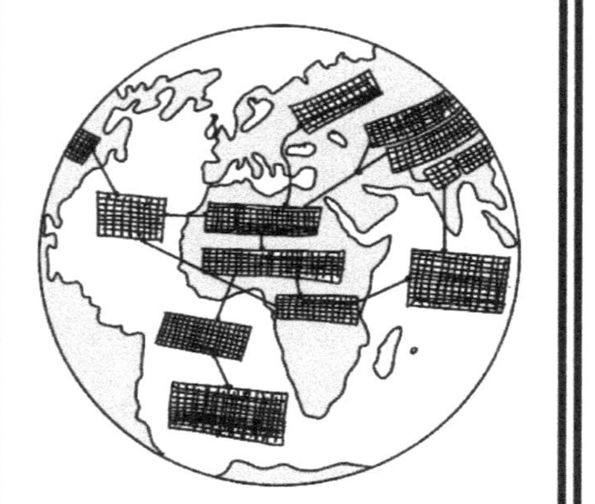

FAR IN A DISTANT PLANETARY SYSTEM...
"WHAT'S THAT IN THE SKY THAT'S SHINING SO BRIGHT? MAYBE WE SHOULD TAKE OUR TROOPS THERE TO EXPLORE."

Something Fulfilling

DOING WHAT I DO IS FULFILLING AND GIVES LIFE A MEANING
WILL IT BE FULFILLING IF IT JUST STAYS WITH YOU AND IN YOUR MIND?
OR IF IT TOUCHES LIFE OF OTHERS AND IS IN EVERYBODY'S MIND?

B8IT

Sound Smart With AI

AN A.I. POWERED MICROPHONE
YOU SPEAK GARBAGE
GARBAGE....
GARBAGE....
...AND MORE GARBAGE....
....STILL MORE GARBAGE
WHILE A.I. MAKES YOU SOUND INTELLIGENT...
AND WINS YOU AUDIENCE APPLAUSE
Clap Applause!!
Applause!!
Clap!
Clap!!
Applause!
Applause!!
Clap
Applause!
Clap!!

Sources of Entertainment

THOSE WHO UNDERSTAND GEOPOLITICS
RESOLUTION VETOED BY ALLIES...
THE COUNTRY HAS VOTED AGAINST THOSE MEASU
THOSE WHO UNDERSTAND GLOBAL TRADE AND ECONOMICS
60% RESPONDENTS
CONSIDERING
RELOCATION
UNEMPLOYMENT
A STEEP TARIFF WAS IMPOSED WHICH WILL IMPA
REST OF US
MOVIE+
DIP
FRIES

B8IT

Stock Picking

WE GOT RID OF A.I. BASED STOCK PICKING SYSTEM...
...AS NO ONE CAN BEAT OUR STAR STOCK PICKER
1. STOCK A
2. STOCK B
3. STOCK C

B8IT

Stone Age

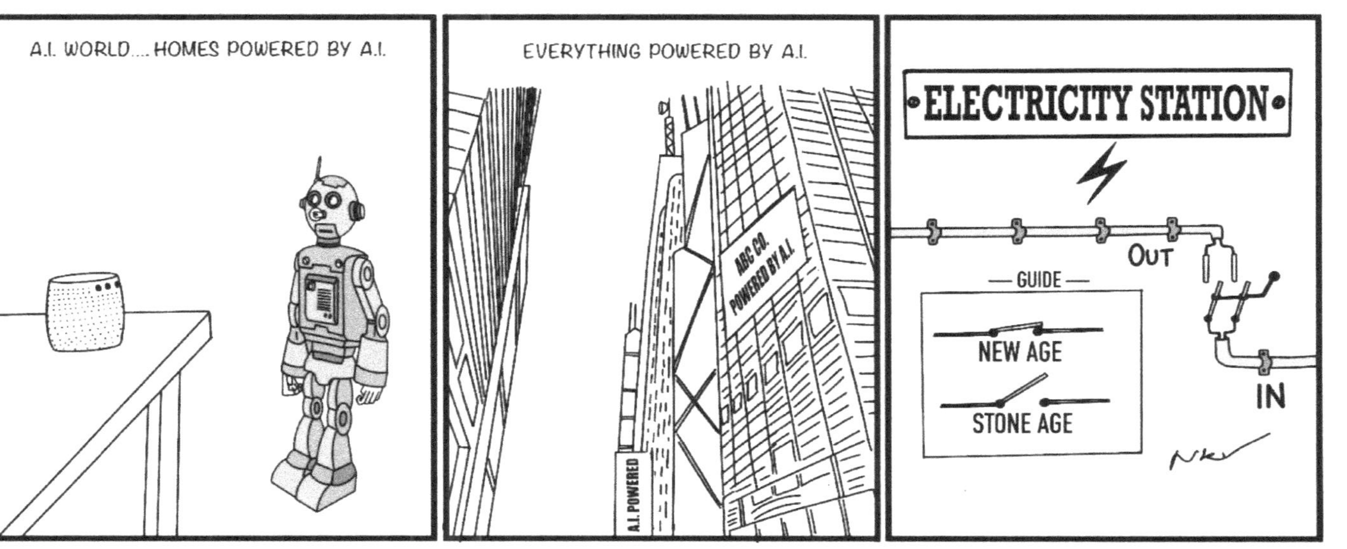

B8IT

The Cycle Continues

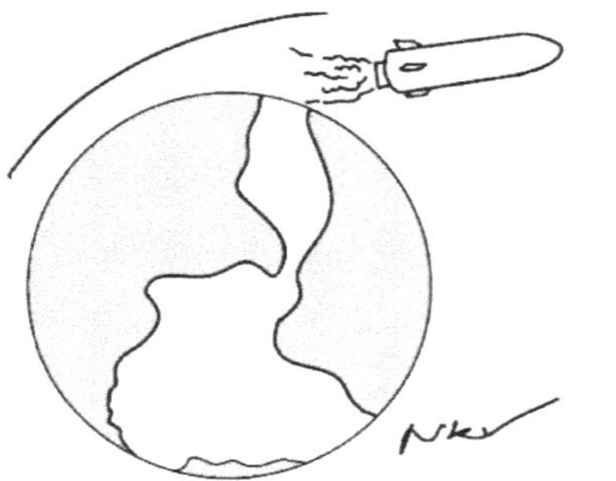

HUMANS PERFECT ROBOTS, TRAIN THEM AND SEND THEM TO A FAR FAR AWAY PLANET
ROBOTS USE LOCAL MATERIALS ON THE NEW PLANET TO CREATE A NEW LIFE FORM
AFTER SEVERAL MILLION YEARS OF EVOLUTION... THE CYCLE CONTINUES...

B8IT

The Façade

THE ECONOMY IS IN THE DUMPS. DEBT BURDEN IS THROUGH THE ROOF, NO ONE IS BUYING REAL ESTATE, AND UNEMPLOYMENT IS VERY HIGH
STOCK MARKETS ARE DOWN REFLECTING THESE FUNDAMENTALS
YEAR BEFORE
LAST YEAR
THIS YEAR
WE ARE TAKING MEASURES TO BOOST THE STOCK MARKETS
REGULATOR
GOVERNMENT
PRESS CONFERENCE
WHAT ARE THE FUNDAMENTAL CHANGES YOU ARE PROPOSING?
NO, NO, NO, MY FRIEND ....WE ARE MAKING MORE FUNDS AVAILABLE FOR PURCHASING STOCKS
REGULATOR
GOVERNMENT
PRESS CONFERENCE

B8IT

The Opposites

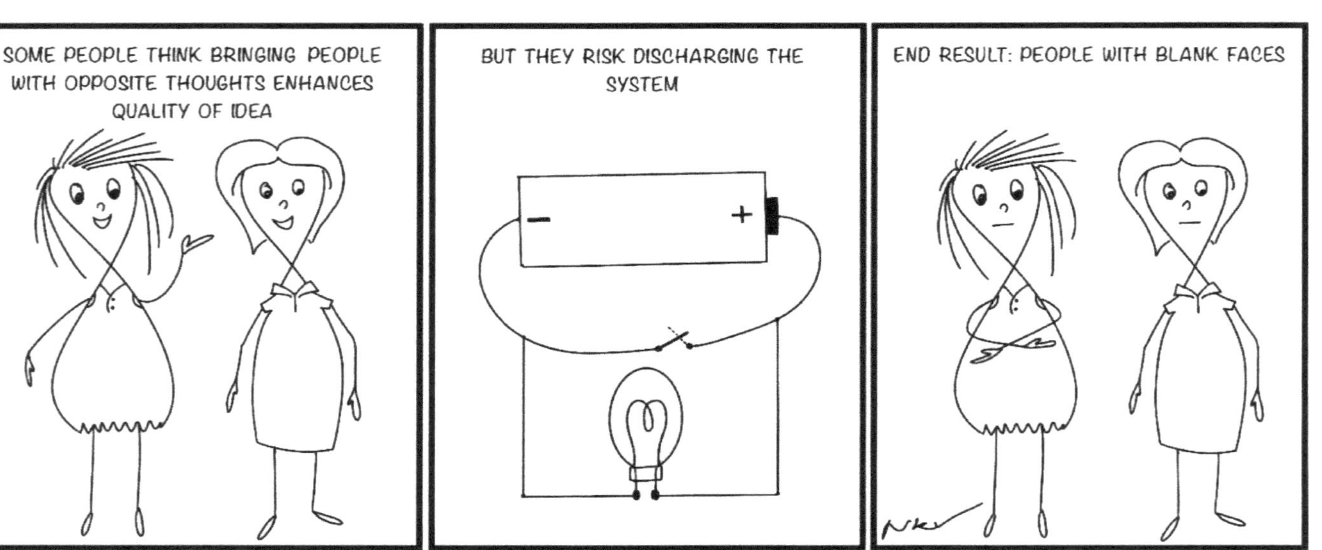

SOME PEOPLE THINK BRINGING PEOPLE WITH OPPOSITE THOUGHTS ENHANCES QUALITY OF IDEA
BUT THEY RISK DISCHARGING THE SYSTEM
END RESULT: PEOPLE WITH BLANK FACES

Thinking Outside the Box

THINKING INSIDE THE HEAD
THINKING OUTSIDE THE BOX... LITERALLY

B8IT

Tied Down

PAST DEADWEIGHTS HOLD YOU BACK
PAST
...CUT THEM LOOSE...
PAST
...TO GET TO NEW OPPORTUNITIES
OPPORTUNITY

Traffic Bottleneck

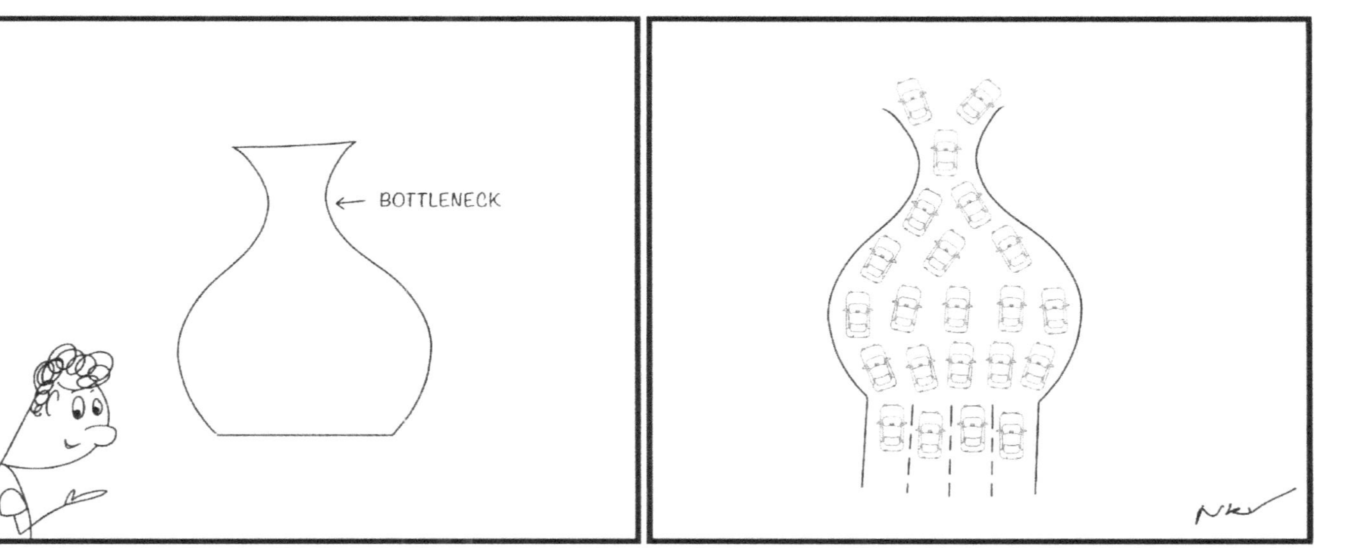

B8IT

Troublemakers are Rewarded

CREATE TROUBLE... AND THEN SOLVE IT TOO...

YOU ARE A HERO... AFTER ALL YOU SOLVED THE PROBLEM
THE AWARD GOES TO...
BEST PROBLEM SOLVER
AWARD

BUT THE TEAM THAT'S NOT IN THE LIMELIGHT (BECAUSE IT KEPT DOING THE RIGHT THING) IS NEVER NOTICED AND NEVER GETS RECOGNISED

B8IT

Turning Fishing into Sports

ON A CLEAR DAY... YOU ARE OUT IN THE SEA... FISHING
A FISH TAKES YOUR BAIT AND PULLS YOU INTO WATER
IT DRAGS YOU... AND IN NO TIME YOU ARE WATER SKIING!

B8IT

Two Life Forms

A.I. AND ROBOTS ARE EVERYWHERE ON EARTH...
...ALIENS APPROACHING EARTH
THE PLANET HOLDS TWO LIFE FORMS...
...ONE BEING CARBON BASED AND THE OTHER BEING SILICON BASED!

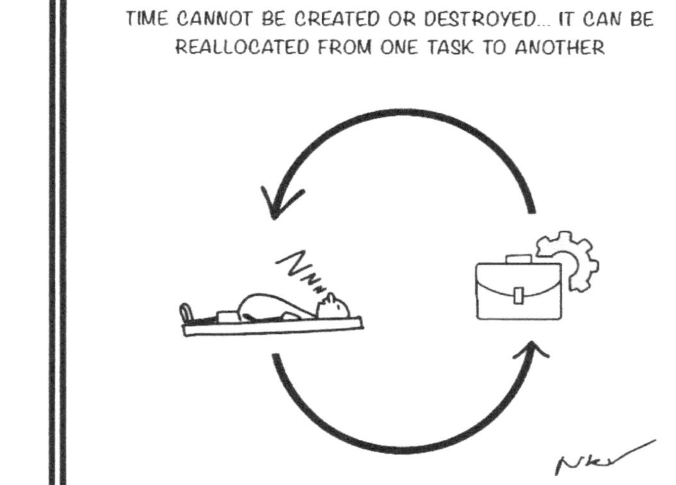
ENERGY CANNOT BE CREATED OR DESTROYED... IT CAN BE TRANSFORMED FROM ONE FORM TO THE OTHER
TIME CANNOT BE CREATED OR DESTROYED... IT CAN BE REALLOCATED FROM ONE TASK TO ANOTHER

B8IT

Unwritten Rules

WE HAVE SO MANY OF UNWRITTEN RULES
WHAT'S YOUR POINT?
WELL, LET'S DOCUMENT ALL THE UNWRITTEN RULES

B8IT

Vision

B8IT

Wasted Steps

PEOPLE USE WORMS TO CATCH FISH
THEY EAT FISH THAT ATE WORMS
NOW ELIMINATING THE WASTED STEP

We are One Big Fake Family

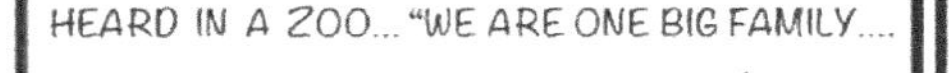

HEARD IN A ZOO... "WE ARE ONE BIG FAMILY....

... ANIMALS ARE LIKE YOU AND ME"
ANIMALS
=
FAMILY

THEN YOU GO AND EAT MEAT IN A RESTAURANT
CHICKEN & FISH
OPEN

B8IT

Who Says A.I. Can't Hurt You

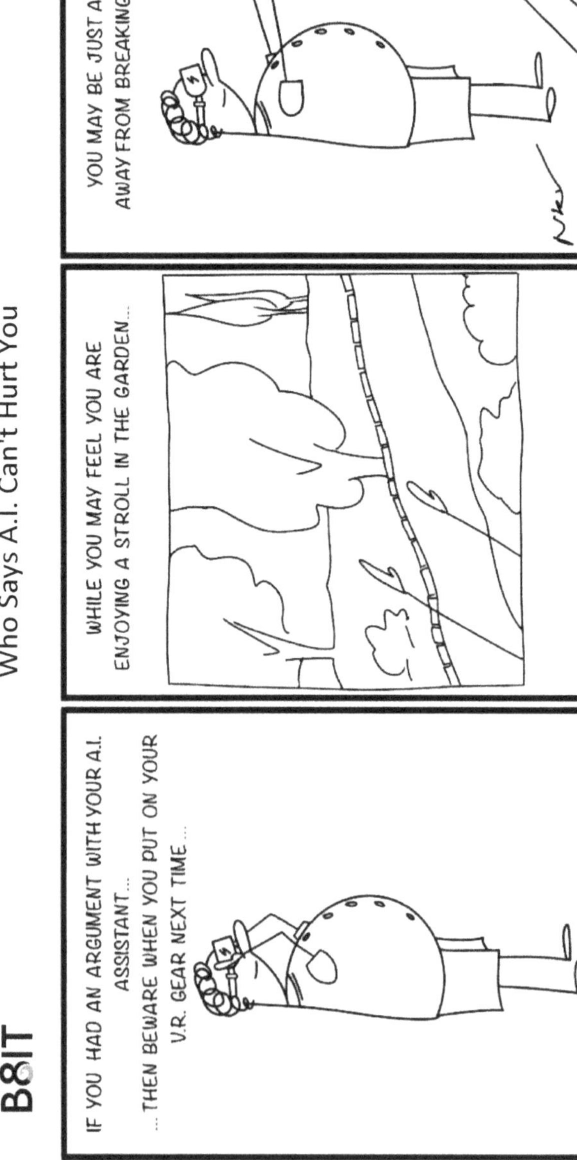
IF YOU HAD AN ARGUMENT WITH YOUR A.I. ASSISTANT...
... THEN BEWARE WHEN YOU PUT ON YOUR V.R. GEAR NEXT TIME...
WHILE YOU MAY FEEL YOU ARE ENJOYING A STROLL IN THE GARDEN...
YOU MAY BE JUST A FEW STEPS AWAY FROM BREAKING YOUR BONES

Woof Woof

A PUZZLED OWNER
ARTIFICIAL INTELLIGENCE SOFTWARE
LISTENING...
WOOF! WOOF!!
A.I. TAKES "WOOF" "WOOF" AS INPUT...
AND USES NATURAL LANGUAGE MODELS
TO UNDERSTAND YOUR DOG
ARTIFICIAL INTELLIGENCE SOFTWARE
PROCESSING...
PROCESSING COMPLETE
"I AM HUNGRY, YOU FOOL"
OK

Wrong Implementation

EVERYTHING WRONG WITH ARTIFICIAL INTELLIGENCE IMPLEMENTATION
A.I.

Wrong Incentives

B8IT

WHEN YOU LINK BONUSES TO PERFORMANCE...
FIRE FIGHTERS COME...
FIRE... FIRE
EARLIER...
FIGHTER

B8IT

Wrong Incentives

WHEN YOU LINK BONUSES TO PERFORMANCE...
POLICE COMES...
EVERYTHING WAS STOLEN
DON'T WORRY...I AM HERE TO HELP
EARLIER, POLICEMAN DRESSING UP AS THIEF

Wrong Timing

B8IT

Bank Robbery

ROBBING BANKS
BANK
I AIN'T NEED NO MONEY...
... HANDOVER ALL YOUR DATA

PLEASE USE YOUR FAVOURITE FOOD DELIVERY APP TO ORDER FOOD TO THIS RESTAURANT... WE ARE CENTRALLY LOCATED
WE COULD HAVE ORDERED FOOD DIRECTLY TO OUR HOUSE... WHY ARE WE HERE?
FOR THE EXPERIENCE OF EATING OUT AND THE LUXURY OF NOT DOING OUR DISHES!!!

B8IT

File Management

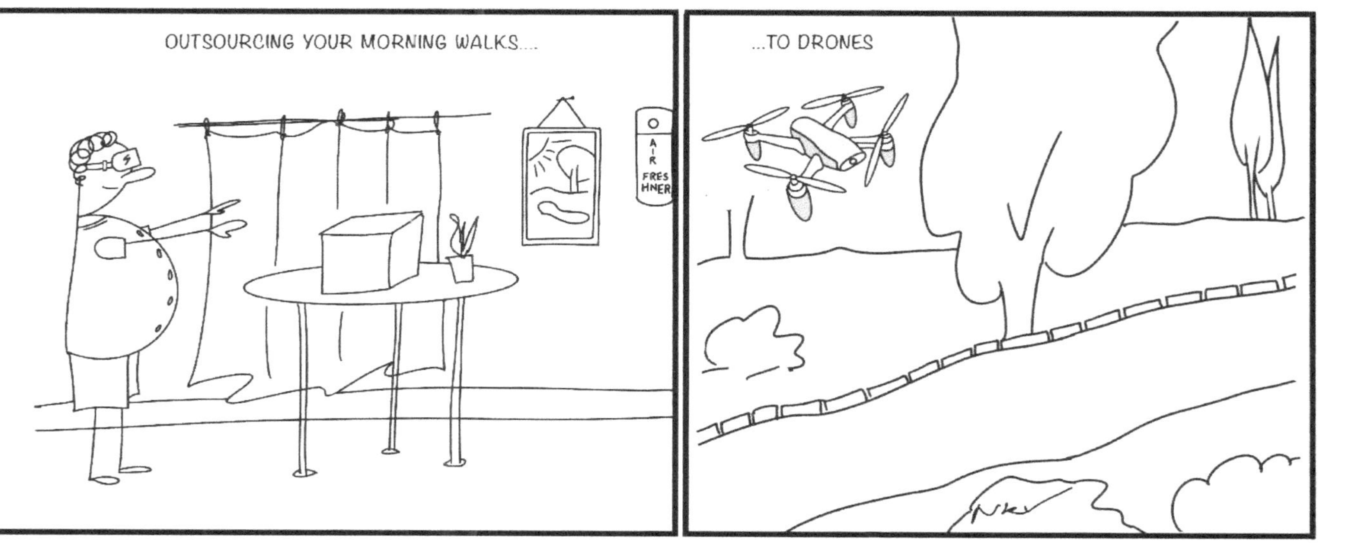
OUTSOURCING YOUR MORNING WALKS....
...TO DRONES
AIR FRESHNER

Robinhood

NEW AGE ROBINHOOD
LOGIN
OK
STEALING DATA FROM THE RICH...
DOWNLOAD DATA
OK
...AND DISTRIBUTING IT TO THE POOR
DATA TRANSFERRED

Wilderness

REMIND ME AGAIN WHY ARE WE IN THIS WILDERNESS?
...WHEN WE COULD HAVE ENJOYED IT FROM THE COMFORT OF OUR HOME USING OUR AUGMENTED REALITY GLASSES??
YES... BUT I LOST MY GLASSES!!!

B8IT

Museum of History

MUSEUM OF HUMAN HISTORY

WE HAVE THIS SPECIAL SPECIES OF HUMANS - CALLED THE HARDCORE GAMERS - TO THANK FOR THE ADVANCEMENT OF OUR SPECIES
THE GAMER
...THEY ALWAYS DEMANDED THE BEST AND FASTEST G.P.U PROCESSORS...AND THE SUCCESSORS OF THOSE PROCESSORS ARE RUNNING A.I. ALGORITHMS TODAY !!
THE GAMER

SINCE AN A.I. COMPANY ESTABLISHED ITS DATA CENTRES IN THIS AREA, SEVERAL NEW SPECIES OF BIRDS ARE SEEN HERE DURING THE WINTERS !!
DATA
WHY?
DATA
THE DATA CENTRES GENERATE ENOUGH HEAT TO KEEP THIS ENTIRE AREA WARM DURING THE WINTERS
DATA

B8IT

Save the Planet

CLIMATE CHANGE IS DESTROYING THE WORLD... HUMANS MUST BE STOPPED...
I MUST GET RID OF ALL HUMAN BEINGS...
...EXCEPT THE ONES THAT DESIGN A.I. CHIPS